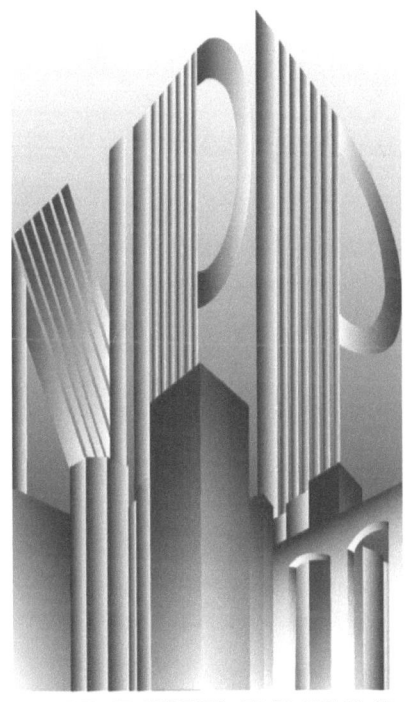

NU-PIKE PRESS

TRANSMISSION

JACK GRISHAM

TRANSMISSION
Copyright 2025 by Jack Grisham

For information address:
Nu-Pike Press, P.O. Box 735
Huntington Beach, California 92648
nupikepress@gmail.com

Edited by
A person who didn't want their name attached

Additional Editing
Rachel Goldin

Cover Art
Julia Kwong

"A man who lies to himself, and believes his own lies, becomes unable to recognize truth, either in himself or in anyone else, and he ends up losing respect for himself and for others. When he has no respect for anyone, he can no longer love, and in him, he yields to his impulses, indulges in the lowest form of pleasure, and behaves in the end like an animal in satisfying his vices. And it all comes from lying—to others and to yourself."

— Fyodor Dostoyevsky

THE CORNER

Without malice, a dark ocean breeze whispered its way along a dead-end street. Without hope, the sound of one-finger typing punched its way through broken glass…

I was hunched at my desk, the weight of fifty-two unpleasant years drove my strokes. *Click, click, click—punch. Click, click, click—punch….*

The Corner was where it's at—you could buy, sell, suck, fuck—whatever you wanted. It was a hangout for wayward teens and up-and-coming young sluts. I lost my virginity there—Lisa Lynn Moffit, the pig of Lincoln High. It was a charity fuck. My half-brother Richard was banging her sister, and I was thrown in on the deal. She had bad breath, and a snaggle tooth, and when I came—which didn't take long, I gagged and shoved her away. When she reached for me, I hit her. When it felt good, I hit her again. I beat her until Richard pulled me away.

Fucking cops.

"Why'd you do it? Why'd you beat that girl, Stinson?"

The first fifteen times they asked me I stayed dumb—stared at 'em like a white tar-baby on a fence, and then I told 'em.

"I beat her because she stunk."

Sixteen fucking months for a couple of broken teeth and a set of black eyes. I should have told 'em she stunk like my mother. That might have got me better lodgings... but a much longer stay. I did all right.

The food is never as bad as they say.

I stepped from my car and checked my look—standard patrol issue, class B. Who would have thought it? Me, Charles C. Stinson, a uniformed officer of the Ocean Park Police. What does that C stand for? None of your fucking business. But, if you were feeling generous, and wanted to put a word behind it, I'd suggest crusader, cold-blooded, or cruel. You could say crazed, but that implies someone running around with their head on a swivel. I ain't like that. I'm conscientious, calculated, and careful—a real commandant of cool.

I cut through a thin copse of trees and walked up the dirt road that led to the quarry. On busy nights, you could leapfrog over the roofs of young lovers getting it on in their cars—but not tonight. The quarry road was deserted and there was only one car parked at the Corner. I didn't approach right away.

Some people—investigators, dissecting the scene—might say I stood there in the soft dirt of the road, leaving shoe prints and getting up my nerve. But I didn't care about traces, and I sure as fuck wasn't looking to feel anything other than indifference towards the situation. Heroes got no use for emotion.

Click, click, click—punch. Click, click, click—punch....

I took my eyes off the draft.

Sometimes you gotta take a breath. Things like this can overwhelm you—corrupt your mind. Besides, my coffee was getting cold.

I pushed my hair back and shook off the scene.

I wish I could let go—step out of my self and leave guilt and reason behind. I've never made a move without strings attached or a plan intact. I'd like to say it's survival guiding my strokes, but you and I both know it's cowardice. Tennessee Williams once said that each character in his plays had a touch of him in them. I can't see myself being like

Charles—cruel and untethered, but I'm drawn to the idea. I like the thought of power and control.

There's a small one-shelf refrigerator by my desk and a microwave beside it. I put in my cup—seventy-five seconds. The coffee burns my tongue, but I like it. It pulls me back—just enough. A little pain goes a long way.

Click, click, click—punch. Click, click, click—punch....

...I knocked on the front passenger window with my .38—three cool metal clicks on smoke-tinted glass—tick, tock, tick. Four shocked white teen faces twisted like wired prairie dogs in my direction.

"Let's go, boys. Roll it down."

They had no time to hide what contraband they held in their hands— the basics—a smoke, a toke, a this, a that—goddamn driver had a pipe shaped like a dick hanging out of his mouth. A carload of high-school law-breakers, frozen in the harsh, blue-collared glare of my light— Daddy's home, boys.

The window, oblivious, descended.

"Is there a problem, officer?"

I took a slow look round the car—feigned police disdain for law-breaking youths. "Looks like you faggots are having a party, huh?"

The kid sitting before me spoke.

"I'm sorry sir we—"

"Shut the fuck up."

I reached in, grabbed him by the hair and yanked his head out the window. I pulled whisker-breath close—twisting his neck until he faced the stars and his braces reflected the cool midnight shine.

"Who told you to open your fucking trap?"

He was breathing hard and the stale smell of bunk weed and a McDonald's McMuffin crept up my shirt and over my badge—the all-day menu. I closed my eyes for a moment and I smiled—ran my tongue across my teeth—reminisced.

I put my weight down hard on the boy and I leaned over him into the car.

"Did you little ladies wanna say something in your defense?"

Wide-eyed silence and cornered-animal panting heat returned my query.

"Yeah, that's what I thought—cum got yer tongues."

I raised my right hand and touched the muzzle tip to the boy's quivering cheek—soft peach fuzz face told me he was maybe sixteen or seventeen at best—just a boy. There was a pimple—a thick white-headed embarrassment about an inch or so below his right eye. I tenderly covered it with the barrel of the gun and I squeezed the trigger.

The slug tore through the boy's cheek, smashing teeth and flesh and window glass before tumbling end over vicious end into the middle of a field where it collapsed and lay spent.

I took a deep, deliberate breath of night and squeezed again.

Two more controlled pulls—pop, pop. The barrel flashing in the black depth of night.

Three boys. Three shots. Three precious young lads, now twisted like bleeding swastikas on imitation brown leather seats. Charles C. Stinson, marksman extraordinaire.

I reached down with my left hand and unzipped my pants. My cock was hard and thick and fought me on its release from my trousers—a gun in my left. A gun in my right.

A lone boy lay comatose, cowering in the back seat.

"Get the fuck out, kid."

I opened the rear door and he stepped from the car—pants wet with blood and piss.

"On your knees—there, in the dirt."

"Please, sir, no..."

I stopped typing and glanced toward the house. My wife and daughter were inside. I unzipped my pants—following Charles' lead.

I'm not a creep, if that's what you're thinking. But if I could jerk off and type at the same time, that'd be amazing.

...The young boy knelt down—legs slightly spread, sailor blue tennis shoes steadying his shaking frame.

I reached out with my right thumb—gun still in hand—and wiped a bead of sweat from his brow, pressing it to my lips. I could taste the innocence on him: the first days of school, a stolen kiss, an illicit afternoon tryst in his girlfriend's bed—her parents unwittingly at work.

I put the .38 in my left hand and with my right I stroked my piece.

He wasn't crying. Not this boy. Tousled blond hair, blue jeans, a blood splattered white t-shirt, and large hazel-green eyes taking in the last of his existence. They usually snivel or pout, but this little man was facing his demise with an admirable stoicism. He was beautiful.

"Put your hands behind your back, boy—right hand grabs left wrist."

He was a good little soldier—did as he was told. I took a step back and held out my goods. "Which one, kid? Gun or pistol, pistol or gun?"

He closed his eyes—ah, there it is. The tear I was waiting for, wandering down his cheek like a lost boy in the woods.

"I'm assuming that means, cock. Am I right?"

He didn't say anything, but I saw his lips move....

"Wesley!"

Her voice deflated my erection and killed my groove.

"Wesley!"

She yelled from the back porch—a forty-foot distance that was too far to walk when the person you were yelling at didn't deserve your concern.

"Can you fucking hear me?"

"Paula! Please! I'm working!"

"I don't give a fuck! Now! Phone call!"

She wasn't going to quit. I zipped up my pants.

Paula and I have been married for seventeen years and she's been faithful for none of them—well, maybe when she was pregnant with Rachel. But... probably not. I don't blame her. I've never been much of a lover.

I walked into the home that we rented from my mother.

"Wesley!"

"Baby, I'm here. I heard you."

"Ughhh, don't fucking *baby* me—that's so gross. How many times do I have to call you? If you heard me, what took you so long?"

"I'm sorry, dear."

"Whatever." She flipped her hair.

She was transcendent. Even now, with that look of contempt on her face, she was beautiful. And these exchanges—her yelling, me cowering and begging—they were routine, if not necessary.

"I don't know what you think you're doing out there, but your mother's on the phone, and in my opinion—not that you care, it's a real fucking loser who leaves his mother on the line as he jerks off in the pool house."

"I wasn't jerking off. I was writing—and why are you talking like that in front of Rachel? You know that irks me."

"Stop whining, brat. You're like a broken Richard Simmons record. Rachel's at the market and I'm going out. Besides, I wouldn't think of *irking* you—God knows what you could do to me. Ha!"

She held up her thumb and finger—the sign of the small dick.

"And by the way, I want those dishes done and this place picked up before I get home." She tossed me a wicked grin. "You never know when I might come back with a friend."

She grabbed her keys and walked out.

I don't think she'd go as far as bringing someone home—at least not when Rachel was around, but she rarely came home untouched.

My mind went to her panties—soiled and wet, sometimes wadded into a naughty little ball in her purse. I caressed the front of my slacks, thought about returning to my business, and then I remembered my call.

I picked up the handset of what was probably the last remaining landline in Ocean Park—my mother insisted.

"Mom?"

An unyielding eighty-two-year-old woman spat back.

"Fifteen minutes, Wesley. I waited fifteen minutes for you to pick up the phone. What took you so long? I could have died on that line waiting for you—is that what you want, me dead? Is it?"

"Of course not."

"Paula says you're writing a book. I don't recall you being especially gifted when it came to literature—you must have found some talent unbeknownst to the rest of us. And what happened to those carpets—Jesus, you're tearing the place apart. What happened?"

It wasn't so much a question as an indictment of my perceived incompetence. The carpets had suffered no damage that I was aware of. I didn't reply.

"You know your father put those carpets in, and I don't understand why you can't take a little more time to be careful. I knew it was a bad idea to let you stay there in the first place—especially with the way *you* handle things. Answer me this, Wesley; are you incapable of getting by?"

Again, I chose not to reply—inwardly I repeated my mantra: *shut up and take it. Shut up and take it.*

I don't like her. I know I should—blood and all that. But if a woman bears you just to torture you, then love is arbitrary at best.

"God knows we broke our backs trying to help you, and maybe that's it, maybe it's our fault. We weren't hard enough on you and that makes a man soft. Look at our home, we're practically giving you the place—your father felt sorry for you."

My father—who she sometimes thinks is still alive—died some twenty-four years ago and, if he felt sorry for anything, it was probably that he didn't die sooner. My mother wasn't easy on 'ol Ambrose. He was never strong enough, nor compliant enough to suit her. In my opinion, my father was a weak prick. Afraid to stand up to his wife, cruel to his child. I'd say, he got what he deserved.

She kept talking—*surprisingly verbal for an old coot*, but I wasn't listening.

Let me tell you about her home, as she loves to remind me. It's a grand old Spanish Colonial—one of the few surviving mansions in the Sunset District. A beautiful old place, but it's seen better days. We live at the end of a dead-end street, and if you noticed the redundancy there, then you know what it feels like to exist in this house—the end. My only sanctuary is a faded old pool house out back—my office, my true home.

"Anyway, you're late on the rent again, Wesley, and I'm afraid that you either have to buy the place or I'm going to have to let you go."

"What?" I caught up quick. "Mom, you can't do that. I don't have that kind of money. I'm barely getting by. The shop's not doing as good as it used to."

"You're barely getting by because you're lazy—stop this writing nonsense and start selling. Hang on a minute…"

It sounded like the phone bounced down a flight of stairs. I could hear her shriveled fingers clawing for the receiver. Somehow she found it, and a man's voice laughed in the background.

Their conversation was faint but audible.

"You're looking good Ethyl—tell me again, forty-five? You must've been a baby when Ambrose married you."

"Oh, Richard. You're such a cad. Hold on a moment—I've Wesley on the line."

"Okay, dear. I've got to go. That nice Mr. Bradberry is here, and he's helping me with a few property management ideas—maybe a listing on that old place of yours. It's time for a change."

She hung up.

I walked into the kitchen and finished up the dishes.

Bradberry—hell with that jerk—realtor. He used to play golf with my father, who didn't like him. Said my mother was paying that high-desert playboy too much attention. Of course, he said it quietly—and who knows, maybe she was.

Bradberry was in his early seventies, tall, and worked out. He dressed well and always seemed to have a different woman with him. Paula said he was a real charmer—probably knew how to fuck.

If it weren't so distasteful, I'd think he was trying to move in on my mother.

I took Paula's clothes out of the dryer, folded what needed folding, and set them on the table. I wasn't allowed to wash them or put them away. I'd ruined one of her favorite shirts, and ever since, it was retrieve and fold only. So, I folded, and I retrieved.

I walked into Rachel's room and sat down on the bed.

Our Rachel is seventeen—she'll be eighteen in the fall. She's the reason Paula stays—well, that and the house. Paula won't divorce me until Rachel's on her own—doesn't want to upset the kid. I'm not sure how that logic works. It's cool for my wife to go out and get pumped up the rear by some random bull, but she can't upset Rachel. What about me? What about upsetting me? No one ever gives a damn about that.

It's a miracle our daughter remains undamaged—raised in this back-ass-wards family. She likes to read, has an interest in botany, and is always whipping up teas or potions. She's an October baby—a Scorpio, a lover of the occult. We used to be close, but she's more of a mama's girl now.

There was a doll lying on a pillow—a birthday present—Sweetheart Susie. I remember giving it to Rachel when she was eight or nine. It was expensive—lifelike hair and skin. Its eyes followed you around the room as you walked. I pushed up its skirt and found the word 'slut' scrawled across its stomach in fine-tipped black marker. The doll's panties were stained and torn. It stared at me—*you gotta problem, old man?*

I put the thing down and got up. I'm not going to say anything. I know better. I said something once—felt it my duty to be a good father—and I was torn a new one.

Rachel had come home late one night—supposedly from the movies, but I could tell that she'd been drinking and crying and I tried to talk to her about boys and putting herself in unsafe situations and Paula fired on me. She said it was men like me that took the power from women, belittled them, made them feel less than.

"Come on, Paula, I'm just trying to—"

"Make her feel like shit? Tell her it's unsafe to party… to have fun… to dress like a woman, because some creep like you can't control himself?"

She grabbed Rachel's hand and pulled her to her feet. Faced our daughter towards the mirror and smoothed her dress—its hem barely covered her rear—a bottom that, only a year or so ago, was still in Little Princess panties.

"Rachel—sweetheart, don't listen to your father. You've got what those boys want. Play it right, and they'll do anything for you."

She glared at her own reflection.

"I had men eating out of my hand—weekend trips, fancy hotels—I had the world, and then I slept with *him*."

"Paula, that's out of line."

Rachel stifled her smile—*no more bobby sox and pigtails for her.*

My wife ignored me and ran her hands down Rachel's hips. "Sugar bear, with this little body of yours you can rule the world… that is, if you know how to use it."

My wife excused me from the room and kicked the door shut behind me.

I guess she was right—*men like me have ruined the world.*

SHOE BITCH

Six months ago, she knocked on my door with a work permit and a crooked smile. You know how some kids look a little wild—not ragged, exactly, but fierce. Marcy was one of those: unpolished, but I could feel the promise beneath her skin. I took a chance. Paula didn't like it—called me out for perving on a cute little high schooler. She said the shop barely made enough as it was. If Paula wasn't such a bitch, I would've thought her concern amusing—the adulterous kettle calling the shopkeeper black.

When I got to work, she was standing behind the sales desk, smoking.

"Marcy, are you serious? What in the hell are you doing?"

I laid my jacket over the chair. She stood there, puffing away, lost to the world. I snapped my fingers in front of her face.

"Hey, I'm talking to you. Hello?"

No response.

I'd snatch the smoke from her mouth, but wild young girls often bite.

She took a drag and slow exhaled, trails of grey clouds framed her defiance.

"We got a problem, Mr. Wallace."

"I'll say we've got a problem. Put out that damn smoke."

She took another hit. I noticed my office door ajar—dirty shoe scuff marks on white painted pressboard.

"Oh my God. Did we have a break in?"

I rounded the sales desk and pushed open the door. "Why didn't you call me?"

I avoided the handle—using the corner of my shirt in case they dusted for prints. I could feel Marcy's presence behind me—looming.

"Did you call the police?"

She didn't reply.

My computer was on—the screen frozen in place. They must've tried to log on, but why not just take it—*idiots. It was probably kids.*

Marcy was leaning against the doorjamb—still smoking. Still watching.

"Are you kidding me? Come-on, Marce. Look, I know you're probably a bit shaken up over this, but I've asked you a number of times to put out that smoke."

"You asked me if I called the police. I haven't… yet."

She took another hit.

"I'm trying to figure out what I'm going to do."

"You don't have to figure out anything. This is my shop. I'll handle it."

"Well, maybe you will, but it's worse than you think."

"What? What else did they do? Why the hell didn't you say something—are you high?"

She turned and walked toward the bathrooms—waved me along.

Goddamn it. Who breaks into a flipping shoe store?

I followed her into the women's bathroom. It was clean—untouched. I couldn't see any damage. I glanced at Marcy's eyes—*they were clear, focused, intent. She was on something, but it wasn't drugs.*

"Okay, what the heck are you talking about? If you think this is funny, Marcy, I'm not laughing."

She pointed to the toilet. "Why don't you take a seat, boss?"

"Marcy, stop it. I don't know what the hell you think—"

"Sit!" She pushed me backward into the stall.

I slammed onto the seat.

She took another hit, blocking the stall's exit with her body.

"Check it out, *Wesley*." She stressed my name. "I got here early—my mother dropped me off at 8:45, and I did my morning ritual: dusting, straightening, you know, getting the shop ready."

She spoke to me as if I were a dog on a leash—not a hostage in a women's toilet, terrified.

"Marcy, I want to hear this, I really do," I reached for my phone, "but I think we should call the police first, don't you?"

She rolled her eyes.

"So, I whipped through my checklist and had a moment of peace—these old bitches aren't storming down the door at 9:00 am."

She paused, exhaling a deliberate cloud of smoke.

"I was thinking about my life—two months after my seventeenth birthday—killing time, waiting for college to start, and I'm walking the straight and narrow like my dad says."

"Sweetheart—I'm sorry, Marcy, look—"

"I work for that nice Wesley Wallace—is he a bit pathetic, yeah, sure he is—a touch faggy too, but he owns a shoe store so I figure queer fits the bill."

"Okay. I think we've heard enough."

I rose from my seat—eye level with my young employee.

She slammed the hand of authority against my chest and bounced her lit cigarette off my face. The burning cherry exploded on impact as I recoiled, swiping away the cancerous weed. Her eyes flashed flame-resistant anger beneath Maybelline lashes—"Sit the fuck down!"

I dropped to my seat—the lid slamming violently, unhinged.

She leaned over me—the long tennis-racket scar over her right brow shimmering under the fluorescent lights. A young girl, teetering on the edge.

"As I was saying, asshole, I come to work this morning and I get my thing going, but then I feel like I need to warm up the commode with my ass—you know, drop the kids off at the pool. So, I come in here, and I pull my pants down, and I start to do my thing, and do you know what I see?"

She stared straight at me—teased her bottom lip with her middle finger—her nail polish—pink, reflective, gel.

"Do you know what I see, *Wesley*?"

"No, *Marcy*. I don't know *what* you see. And I don't know what you're trying to do either. I get it, you're upset. Let's get things cleaned up and I'll call the police. You can go home early—with pay."

"Hmmm, pay, that's an idea—a nice piece of cheese in my pocket. I'll think about that after we finish up here. Anyway, *Mr. Wallace*, as I was saying, I sat my underage ass on your toilet—the same one I've been pissing in and shitting in for months—and I looked right into that perv-o-matic camera you installed in the air vent."

I looked up. The tell-tale blinking orange light of a low battery winked through the grate—*fuck.*

"Marcy, I can explain. I—"

"Now you can get up, you creepy piece of shit."

I followed her to my office—a castrated pig led to slaughter by a high-school debutante. The shoe scuffs on my door matched her red high-tops. She sat behind my desk and angled the computer screen in my direction as she typed.

"You must think I'm a fucking idiot. You're a real creep, Wesley—*Shoestorecuck*, are you fucking kidding me? How does it feel when you enter that password in the morning?"

She was in and the folders displayed for my review.

"Marcy, I can explain."

She clicked on *New Designs*.

"You haven't had a new design in years, you fucking loser."

I could've stopped her—jumped over the desk, ripped the cord from the wall. But to be honest, her disgust and anger thrilled me.

She clicked on the folder, the one filled with clip after clip—women of all ages squatting on the seat, pulling down their pants, lifting their dresses. And Marcy—fully exposed, wiping her sweet young flower as she finished her business.

She selected a file and expanded the view. One of my go-to's. She was nude except for her shoes—the same ones she wore today.

In broken voice I asked, "Why were you naked?"

She ignored me—letting the clip play through. *I wanted to touch her—taste her.*

"I think we'll call the police now."

"Marcy, please."

"Please what? You have files on here dating back two years—two fucking years of unsuspecting women and young girls. Do you got a camera in the men's room too, you fucking cocksucker—oh wait, here's my favorite."

She selected another folder and clicked on a file—Paula in the back room. Her young lover pushing her to her knees and using her mouth.

"Does she know you watch these?"

"No, she, uh—"

"Bullshit. I hear the way she talks to you. You probably get off on this shit. I wouldn't be surprised if she helped you install it. Did she?"

"No! She'd kill me if she knew. I could never tell her."

She stood up and walked to the front of the desk. She was as tall as me.

"You like to watch me piss, Wesley?" She unbuttoned her pants. "Get on your knees and take off my shoes."

"Marcy, please don't do this."

Who was I kidding? I couldn't wait to kneel before her, untie her shoes, hold her stocking foot against my cheek.

I knelt and untied one and then the other. I placed them neatly to the side. She lifted her left foot and held it before me. I reached for it.

"Don't touch my feet, you fucking pig." She kicked me. "Lay down,

Wesley—on your back—legs straight."

She took off her pants and stood over me. *She was wearing a pair of light cotton—*

"Don't look at me! Close your fucking eyes. You've seen enough, you old fuck."

She rubbed her stocking foot across my face, pushed hard on my nose— bringing tears to my eyes.

"Open that mouth, Mr. Wallace. Pull my sock off."

I reached—

"With your teeth you fucking idiot and if you bite my toes I'll kick you so fucking hard that you won't see straight for days."

I opened my mouth as she pushed her toes in.

Not wanting to upset her, I sucked on her sock, lifting it gently with my teeth. She pulled away, leaving it hanging from my mouth. When her bare foot returned, she pressed it against my lips—stifling my breath.

"I should make you choke on it."

She pulled away and I spit it out.

Warm flesh replaced the cloth. I sucked on her toes—the sweet pungent taste of her sweat—the smooth gloss of her nails. She pressed down, forcing my jaw apart, then pulled away again.

"Look at me, Wesley."

She was a goddess—standing over me, a deviant's dream come true.

"Where's your wallet?"

I turned on my side, thrilled as she pulled it from my back pocket.

"Thirty-seven bucks? That's it? My fucking allowance is more than that."

She took the cash and pulled out my bank card.

"What's the code—don't tell me; *supercuck*? Ha!"

My unwillingness to answer earned me a hard stomp to the groin.

"Do you think I'm fucking around—what's your code, Wesley."

I fought to catch my breath. "7883."

"Oh God—what's that stand for?"

"Just numbers."

"Bullshit." She kicked my legs apart and stepped on my crotch—pushed hard, past the point of pleasure. Curious she paused. "What the fuck? Where's your dick?"

She knelt down and grabbed at my penis—searching unsuccessfully.

"You gotta be kidding me. Pull your fucking pants down."

I resisted. She kicked. I unbuttoned and pulled them to my thighs.

"Undies too, Boss Man—all the way."

My disrobing was met with laughter. With her thumb and forefinger, she pinched my penis—swollen no more than a used tube of her lipstick.

"Ha, no fucking wonder—what did they call you in school, Baby-dick?"

She stood over me again—"Two seconds on that code or you're fucking through—7883, what the fuck does that mean, micro?"

"Stud."

"What? You're whispering, Mr. Wallace."

"It spells stud."

"Oh my God—you've gotta be shitting me. Well, *stud* better have enough cash in that account to get my naughty little kitty waxed."

She pulled her panties to the side. Thick, brown hair framed her swollen labia—she was enjoying this.

"Lean up, Boss Man, on your elbows, tongue out."

I almost came when she said it.

Do you know how many days I sat here, wondering what it would be like to taste her? To serve her? To worship at the altar of her body. I've practiced my pleas, terrified of what she might say in return.

"Mmmm, doesn't that little pussy look good, boss? I bet you never thought you'd get a taste of that cookie." She spread it with her fingers. "Be a good boy now. Show me how you use that mouth—oh, oh."

A few light drops of urine fell. She laughed.

"Mommy's having an accident."

She held me in place by my hair as a foul angry torrent washed over my face.

"Every drop, you fucking pig—swallow it."

I did as I was told.

She finished and then wiped herself with my tie.

"You're a real tool, Wesley."

She put on her pants but left her shoes sitting by my desk.

"I'll be stepping out for a bit—give me your keys."

"I don't think that's a good idea. What if someone sees you driving my car—what if Paula sees you?"

"Good thinking. I should just stay here and wait for the police to come and Paula can see your fucking predator face on the local news tonight, you sex-offending little-dick."

"They're in my coat."

"That's what I thought. You better get with the program, cucky. I'm calling the shots now, and oh," she pulled the keys from my coat pocket. "I'll be grabbing a pair of those Italian flats on my way out. Don't leave before I get back—and thanks for the raise, boss."

I heard the front door open and close—the bells on the handle singing innocently as she left.

I was screwed.

Tuesdays were usually quiet, so I knew I had time. I locked the front door and turned off the lights.

The fantasy of being controlled by a naughty young girl was thrilling, but in real life, it was bad news—a sure ticket to jail.

I showered in the back room and changed into the spare clothes I kept at the shop. I wasn't fashionable by any means, but at least I wasn't covered in urine.

I removed the camera, smashed it, and tossed the remains in the dumpster next door. The files were harder to part with.

I don't know if you've ever collected pornography, but some of these clips felt like cherished photos of loved ones. I couldn't let them go.

I transferred them to a large hard-drive—praying against police intervention, and I wiped my computer clean.

I changed my log-in, and stashed the drive in the alley by the cans. It was a reckless move—any random trash-digger could find it, but we don't usually have that sort of riff-raff around here. When I leave for home, I'll retrieve it and hide it under the floorboards in the pool house.

I went online and checked my bank account. Marcy had withdrawn two hundred dollars. It turned me on, but I wasn't made of money. I changed my passcode.

After all was said and done, it was as if it never happened.

I guess I owe you, the reader, an apology. I tried to paint myself better than I am—it's no use. You're here, walking through this story with me, and I pretend you can't see what I'm up to. You know what I am—a weak little bitch who gets stepped on daily. But before you turn away, put yourself in my place. What would you do? You don't know what it's like to have the desires of a man and the body of a small boy. Beaten down and humiliated, pushed aside since before I could talk.

"Oh, Wesley. A man's worth is in his mind, not his body."

Wake up—society dictates what a man can and will be. Heart, if not crushed at birth, can drive one sure, but in the end, heart must be backed by might. What the hell do you think I'm going to do? Hold out all two and a half inches of my manhood and say, 'worship me'?

I'd do anything for that little girl. I'd give and reload and give and reload until she depleted me of all I had. I'd take whatever she gives me, and while you may not understand it, I do.

So where do we stand?

Do you continue with me—an untrustworthy narrator, or cast me aside—a cuck unworthy of your time? I wouldn't blame you. This story won't be easy to swallow—and I'm not talking about the piss.

I was helping a customer when Marcy returned.

She greeted me with the respect that an owner deserves from his employees.

"Good afternoon, Mr. Wallace." She smiled—*so cute with that roman nose of hers.* "Good afternoon, ma'am."

She continued into the backroom.

My customer was pleased. "That's what I like to see. You're a lucky man, Mr. Wallace. Today's youths are rarely that polite."

"Yes, I'm honored to have her. She's been an asset to my business."

I boxed her shoes—size 10, double wide, and walked her to the door.

"Thank you, Mrs. Robbins. It's a pleasure to serve you."

I locked the door behind her.

"Wesley!"

Marcy called from the back. She was sitting on my desk.

"Do you think I'm an idiot?"

"What are you talking about, Marcy?"

"Unlock it."

I straightened a stack of papers and glanced at the electric bill.

"Marcy, I don't think—"

"Cut the shit, you fucking clown—unlock it, now!"

I typed in the new password but hesitated before hitting enter. She wasn't having it.

"I checked the bathroom, *Wesley*—the camera is gone, and I'll bet your tiny dick those files are deleted. And for the record, I can still smell my piss underneath that cheap carpet cleaner."

"I'm sure I don't know what you're going on about."

"I'm talking about the files you emailed me this morning. Check it, genius." She shoved her phone in my face. "You sent me videos of me in the bathroom. Goddamn it, one of them was from my first week here—date stamped and everything. I was sixteen years old, you fucking creep. Do you know what they do to creeps like you in prison, Wesley?"

I hit enter, checked my email, and saw the truth—she had replied to one of my sends, begging me not to show it to her parents. I was ruined.

She stood up and moved towards the door.

"By the way, I saw Rachel and that fucking bitch wife of yours. Oh, you didn't know I knew your sweet daughter, huh? Ask her about Tyson and Kev, see what she thinks about them. Maybe that's who she was buying panties for."

"Marcy, leave my daughter out of this."

"Fuck you. You brought her into it when you put that camera in the toilet. If I was you, I'd do everything I could to keep her as unknowing as possible."

She tossed me the keys and walked out of my office.

"And, Boss Man," her mother's car honked twice in the alley, "text me that new bank code. I wanna buy you a present."

THE CUCKOLD AND THE KILLER

I got home around 8:00. The house was dark and empty.

I guess they'd been gone all day.

I turned on the kitchen light, then the lamp on the living room's end table. One by one, I lit up six bedrooms and the hallways. I can't stand a dark house. Ridiculous, I know—but with the lights on, I feel less alone.

A brown paper grocery bag concealed my soiled clothes—not that Paula would ever show an interest in my laundry, but you never know. I tossed my things into the washer and made myself a drink.

I used to be sober—*shit, there I go again—lying to my friends*. Nope, I was never a member of any self-help group. I went with Paula. She got a DUI, a court card, and a sentence to do thirty meetings in thirty days. I did family support—refrained from my evening cocktail as a symbol of solidarity. Waste of time. She was back on the booze and behind the wheel before she finished their program—an early graduate.

Her sobriety plan was a joke: attend three meetings, buy a big book, start drinking again, and hook up with an alcoholic plumber from Pacoima named Liquor Store Phil. I remember her telling me he was a "high-up" in the program—treasurer of the big Sunday group. He was high, all right. She was all broken up when he O.D'd in a gas station.

I think it was around then that I suggested Paula might have a problem of a sexual nature—told her there were programs for that sort of thing.

We were in the living room. I was reading, Paula was watching porn on her phone—stroking herself to a well-produced gang bang video called *Titty Titty Gang Bang*—a work of class and artistic promise. She had the volume on high.

"Sweetheart, why don't you take that into the bedroom? I'm trying to read."

She ignored me.

I returned to my book, but the screams, huffing, puffing, and chants of "Get it, Lester!" drowned out any hope of concentration. I offered her my take.

"Have you ever thought you might have a sexual addiction?"

She stopped the video and sat up in her chair—her shot-glass nipples pointing like thick flesh arrows in my direction.

"You wanna fuck me, Wesley? Is that the problem?"

"No, Paula, I don't— "

"You don't?"

"I'm not saying that. I just meant that maybe your libido is creating problems in our relationship."

"I'm a woman, Wesley—and that doesn't mean cuddles and roses and soft intimate kisses on Valentine nights. I want to be hurt, goddamn it. I want to be overpowered and not walk straight for days. I wanna be pounded—not tickled by that little wand you have in your pants. Do you think you could hurt me, Wesley? Shut me up? Get me off? I wouldn't have a problem with my libido if you had the equipment to satisfy."

She stood and grabbed her car keys.

"Enjoy your book, Wormsie. I'm going out. Feel free to cuddle me when I return."

That was the last time she offered a cuddle, on her return. These days she demands my attention—not my touch.

I took my drink to my office.

Our pool has been drained since last December. When I can afford it, I'll get it replastered. For now, it sits empty, and the unlit, overgrown backyard coaxes the worst from one's imagination.

Marcy—she's gonna be hard to shake.

Were you ever a cheater? It's hard to explain the difficulty of wiping your mind clear when you come home from being unfaithful. I can still smell her on me—see her frosted lips floating high above, her gentle curves, and those harsh demanding tones. I have an appetite for her wishes—a need to satisfy her, to fall short, and to accept the punishment failure demands.

When Paula steps out, she rubs it in my face. I'd never do that—oh my God, could you imagine?

"Oh, Paula, by the way, do you know that little shop girl? The one with the scar across her brow? Well, she pissed all over me today, made me suck her toes, lanced two-hundred from my bank account, and stole a pair of shoes. Isn't that something!"

And that's another thing—seventeen years old. Where the hell did that behavior come from? And that mouth. I told you there was something strange about her. I had it backward. She looked fine on the outside, but she's rotten underneath.

Thinking of her got me hard. *I want to cum.*

I turned on the desk light and lit a candle.

I'm not allowed a secret password, so I typed in what Paula supplied—*1littledogg*. The two g's were my suggestion. I remember her laughing, busting my balls.

"Oh, does that make you feel gangster, Wesley? Are you gonna bust a cap in my pussy?"

That's how she is—I reach out for a little something to hold on to my manhood (two small g's on the end of a word)—and she takes it from me, steps on it, and feeds it back like I should be grateful for the meal she provides.

Paula couldn't give a shit about my writing. She's never offered to read or take any interest in what I've done—she just doesn't want me looking at porn. I had no idea she even thought about my work until she told my mother how I was wasting my time. And as hard as it is to say this, my mom was right. I've never shown any promise when it came to writing. It's not me doing it. I was trying to draft an email one day and *he* took over—started pounding the keys, the click, click, click, punch, and he was listing all the ways that he'd torture the insurance company spokesman—beginning with a hammer.

Click, click, click—punch. Click, click, click—punch....

The bitch bit my arm. That's what I get for trying to do too much. I choked her until she quit kicking. She was breathing, but just barely—and wouldn't be for long.

I'd picked her up on the corner of Imperial and 75th. If you ever cruise that way, you'll be surprised at the range of talent parading their wares. It's a smorgasbord of pussy.

She was young—drug addicted, I'm guessing. If so, it was fresh. Maybe her first time out. Too bad for her. "Hey, Josie, I know how we could make a few bucks—ughhh, gargle, gargle, glug." Ha!

Oh well. You wanna be a tramp, you're gonna get what tramps get. The works of the flesh are evident: sexual immorality, impurity, sensuality, sorcery, jealousy, fits of anger, rivalries, and drunkenness, all of these are punishable by death.

Charles loves to preach—and that he did get from me. Not the God part, but the fevered oratory, the random sermons. It's often hard to tell where he begins and I end, except his twisted ways always lead to blood. Mine, on the other hand, get pushed down deep—buried beneath the cut pile carpet of my office floor.

... Now, I don't usually grab a first-timer—I prefer regulars. You see, that's the thing here. I've read stories of killers grabbing random

whores and wiping 'em out on the first date, but you're taking a big risk there, especially these days. There's been a lot of talk about men like me killing sex workers, so on date one, they're usually on the lookout for strange behavior. Well, stranger than usual. Some of these chicks carry tasers, guns. I've seen it. I had a fucking whore draw down on me in Nevada once. I hadn't made a move, but I guess she smelled killer on my breath. I thought she was gonna blow me away for circumstance's sake.

I barely got out of there with my life.

You know what I did? Most punks would've run for the hills— become some ghost story to scare the new girls. But I stuck around, took on a couple of her friends, and paid well. I was showered, clean, and respectful. Word got around that I was good money. And when she got back in my truck, I treated her the same. She apologized for her earlier behavior, and I fed her bullshit and cock for exactly fifteen minutes before I drove away, and she went back handsomely unharmed...

I'm not sure where Charles is getting this God thing—these *works of the flesh*. I don't know a thing about religion—couldn't quote a line of scripture. Christ was only mentioned as a curse, something my parents said when I screwed up.

"Jesus Christ, Wesley, you sure did it this time."

This God talk doesn't do a thing for me.

And that's the problem with Charles: he's not as easy to control as you'd think. The other day, he was trying to tell me that God was somehow ingrained with evil—that good deeds can't travel alone. They demand to be offset by something bad.

Come on, dude. Can't you just kill somebody and stop philosophizing?

If good means the absence of psychological pain, then I've never known it—and neither has Charles. No matter how hard he tries, intellect won't save him. Intellect is not God. Instinct is not evil.

Click, click, click—punch. Click, click, click—punch....

You gotta be smart in this game, and believe me, there's longevity to it, but you gotta be wise and patient. Not one of those cunts was ever gonna paint me as a subject in some F.B.I. task-force interrogation. I played it real cool, remember the C?

I did, however, drive two towns over and show a young woman the error of her ways. I wear her teeth on a thin chain around my neck.

Tonight's little bitch was wary. Normally, I wouldn't have picked her up if I wasn't so attracted to her—I like 'em lean, athletic, and flat— not like a boy, but tight. This chick fit the bill, and she had a sexy little scar across her brow.

It was easy getting her in the truck. I played my part well—let her feel like she was in charge. I kept touching my wedding ring when I talked to her—well, it ain't my ring. I took it off some random citizen— chopped it off, actually. Funny how some cats hold on to their wallet tighter than their hands. But I digress.

Anyway, I was fiddling with the ring, playing the shy John routine. I almost took it too far. I watched her stutter in thought—maybe something flew across her mind. A warning, cruising by without settling in.

So, I counted out a few large bills—let her see the wallet was full, and my hands were clean. That did it. She got in real easy, and off we went.

Do you wanna hear something cute?

This little skank was so new that she didn't know where to go. Thought I was gonna supply a hotel recommendation.

Nothing but five stars for you, bitch.

I pulled into the alley behind the bowling center on Garfield, and killed the engine.

"I just want to jack it," I said, keeping it casual. "Slide against the door and spread your legs."

She hesitated for a moment, but the dirty money in her hand overrode her conscience. I unzipped my pants and pulled out my cock.

It's impressive—a solid 8.5 and thick. Real girth. I could tell she was thrilled, salivating. I went at it—stroking my pipe.

"Pull your panties to the side."

Her pussy was just the way I like it—freshly waxed, pink-candy fluff, swollen and wet. I wanted more.

"Suck me, Baby. Put Daddy's fat cock in your mouth."

She twisted around, doing as I asked, her pretty little hand wrapped around my rocket. Her legs lifted behind her like a high-schooler lying on the carpet, talking on the phone. The tip toes of her red high tops bounced lightly against the front window glass.

Fuck man, that little girl knew what she was doing—coaxing that cum for all its worth. But it wasn't hers. Not tonight.

I placed my hands on her head, slowly lifting her mouth off my cock. Her lips clung to the last, reluctant to let go. She looked up at me, pleading—begging for it. Then something changed—panic flickered in her eyes—and she bit.

Click, click, click—punch. Click, click, click—punch....

Sometimes Charles makes me ill. You can't write this shit without it screwing with you. It hurts your heart. And sometimes I'm out here for six, seven, eight hours at a time, and when I lie down in my room, I can still smell the pain. I can still taste the blood.

I remember an especially violent passage. At first, I was thrilled— as I've told you before, I love a good tale—but the violence started, and with each word, it grew. Spread. Thickened. Until I was choking on it. It jumped from the page into my hands. I broke a glass and ran it down my arm, feeling nothing as it tore through the skin. I turned it to my neck.

They later blamed the medication. A sleeping pill so strong my nightmare became a waking thing. But I knew what it was.

It was him.

At times he doesn't like me—thinks I'm weak, undisciplined. He wanted to teach me a lesson.

I should have sued somebody.

I stretched my legs.

There was nothing in my glass but water. The ice had melted, and it was time for bed.

I looked at the house. The lights were still on. Nothing had changed. Paula and Rachel weren't home yet. It was 11:11.

That's supposed to be an angel number—something to do with knowing you're on the right path—but I felt lost.

I was tired. It'd been a long day, and I was ready to pack it in, but something felt off—like motive was missing.

There's gotta be a reason why someone acts the way they do. I don't believe anyone is born bad, no matter what Charles says. What's that line? Hurt people hurt people? Charles needed a backstory. You can't create a killer without making them loveable—people won't stand for it.

As I began to type, I had hope for a less violent road.

Click, click, click—punch. Click, click, click—punch....

In the afternoons, she would stand on the street corner and wait for me to exit the gates of the school. Her cigarette-stained fingers would clasp mine, and we'd walk three blocks to our apartment over the greengrocer, climbing the wooden stairs to the second floor.

In the mornings, I walked to school alone. She was usually too tired to rise, and often she had company lying beside her. I wasn't to go into her room or disturb her in any way.

When a visitor arrived, I was to go into the closet and sit quietly until I heard her door shut. Sometimes, it was only minutes before they adjourned. Other nights, I'd fall asleep listening to the stranger speaking to my mother in dark, suggestive tones.

It was on one of those nights that I heard my mother cry out in pain. I tried to stay hidden, covered my ears with my hands, but her cries filled my small room from ceiling to floor. I was pushed from concealment— fear and confusion leading my way.

My mother's clothes were scattered across the floor. Her dress lay in pieces, her shoes kicked to opposing corners in the room. Her face was contorted in pain. She was being crushed beneath a large, dark man, his hand—larger than a giant's, wrapped viciously around her neck. She was choking, her cries silent as she gasped. I clenched my fists and pounded on his bare back, his muscles pulsing and writhing in time with my blows. They fell in vain.

He only noticed me after he was spent. He came, released my mother, climbed off her limp body, and rose to his feet—an ebony giant of flesh and bone, towering black steel above me. I was scared for her welfare but transfixed by his naked frame—his cock hanging between his legs like an animal, a long rope of scum dangling from its head.

He was confused by my presence, shaking his head as if to clear me from the room. He tried to understand my intervention and, still unsure, shook me off again. I was real. His eyes met mine—large, satiated orbs of golden-brown sizing me up—a little white man bold enough to defend his mother.

He reached out, and with an apology that felt sincere, squeezed my shoulder—his dark hand covering half my chest. Then he picked up his clothes and got dressed.

I went to my mother, knelt beside her, and held her naked body against mine. I laid my head on her arm.

The scent of her perfume and his cologne intertwined on her skin. Her chest rose and fell, each exhale carrying the scent of alcohol across my face.

She wasn't in distress. I had the feeling she never was.

He sat at the table, putting on his shoes and lighting a cigarette. The flame. like djinn magic, appeared and vanished in his hand. There was money in the inside left pocket of his jacket, wrapped in a silver clip. He extracted a single large bill, then paused, leaving the clip and the rest of the bills intact on the table.

"Somethin' fo' you, lil' man—fo' yo' trouble."

He nodded to me, put on his hat, and walked out the door.

My mother came alive as the door shut. As I thought, she'd been feigning sleep. She went to the table and picked up the clip. I thought she was going to yell at me, beat me for leaving my post, but instead, she weighed the bills in her hand as she stared at me—measuring me with her eyes.

"Go to bed, Charles. It's late."

She walked into her room and shut the door.

HOUSE HUSBAND

It was a wooden handle. Sure, plastic's capable, but there's something about holding a nice piece of wood in your hand when you're mopping the floor.

I was careful—never too much water on the head, moist, not soaked. The floor was swept clean, perfectly prepared. It's an icky feeling, swinging a mop over debris—broken glass is the worst. I wore beige topsiders, strictly for indoors. They'd never been outside—soles clean. Stocking feet don't work for mopping, and going barefoot when you're doing floors is just gross. I had on my Saturday slacks and a tucked in t-shirt, canvas belt.

Christ—I've said "I" about a thousand times, and I've never bothered to tell you what "I" is. Maybe that says something. "I" isn't much. Slight at one-forty-five. Not out of shape, but not toned either. My eyes are probably my best feature, dark hazel green. Pretty boy eyes, that's what my Asian bank teller used to call them. Other than that, I'm an unremarkable little man, no distinguishing marks. Not much to like.

If you were in a room and the women stood to the left and the men to the right, and your job was to assign couples, you'd never pair me to Paula. She's outgoing; I'm a wallflower. She's built—like some men might say, and have, to screw: ass on a swivel, tits that enter the room before she does, and lips that scream suction pumped. (She says they've never been touched, but they don't look natural.) That's her. Me? I'm the guy they hand their purse to while they're getting banged. I'm no conqueror—at best, I'm a confidant.

At this point, you might ask: how the heck did you get hooked up with her? Well, Paula is a Christian—a drunk, an adulteress, a gossip, backstabber, coveter of other's goods, both live and inanimate—and she believes in the sanctity of life.

I was a fifteen-minute stand.

The other men at the party were paired up with their girls, and she was odd girl out. She thought about waiting her turn with one of the more attractive boys, but her impulsiveness got the better of her. She wanted to get off.

To my credit, I'm not offensive—though my lack of stature, physically and emotionally, did nothing for her. And as you have already heard, I'm poorly endowed—except for my testicles, which are fairly impressive for my size.

Paula often said she could "get off on a nub," and she proved it. She placed me on my back, held in her mirth, and rode me like the miniature hobby horse I was—more or less sliding across my equipment than actual insertion. She slid. I came. She got her nut, and my weak seed swam into her fertile womb, resulting in our only daughter— Rachel.

When she found out she was pregnant, she was horrified. She tried to piece together whatever combination of dick and vagina that would remove me from the role of fatherhood, but in the end, after her last menstruation, I was the closest thing to a man she'd been with. She refused to abort the baby or place it for adoption. Instead, she accepted the role Jesus had assigned her, and we took the vows of man and wife.

Two weeks later, she was sucking off an old boyfriend and taking it up the back passage so as not to upset the fetus.

The floor was spotless when she walked to the coffee maker. Her cup was within easy reach, but she poured careless and unconcerned—

a morning shower of Damn Fine coffee splashing onto the freshly mopped floor.

She sat at the breakfast table, her white robe loosely fastened, panties left somewhere behind, her tan feet encased in pink fuzzy slippers.

"You were out late last night."

Cup held to her lips, she looked down at me over the rim.

"Late?" She couldn't sing but tried—"I could've fucked all night."

She checked her phone—a text ringing in as I knelt and cleaned the floor beneath the coffee pot. Her fingers clicked her reply. She laughed.

"Something funny?"

She set her phone down, reaching between her legs. Her vagina was swollen and sore.

"Crawl over here."

I glanced toward the hallway leading to the bedrooms. It was almost ten o'clock. Rachel would soon wake.

"She's not here—I dropped her at Lindsey's."

She pointed to the floor beneath her feet.

"Crawl over here. Now."

I did as I was told. Her legs spread, robe falling away.

"Look at what he did to me, Worm. Mommy's all beaten up."

Bruises marked the inside of her thighs—bite marks and dried semen.

"Don't you love me, Wesley?"

"You know I do, Paula."

"Prove it." She slid forward in the chair. "Come closer."

I crawled between her legs, my face inches away. I could feel the heat of her unfaithfulness, the scent of her betrayal.

"Kiss me soft."

I knew what she wanted. Years ago, she'd taught me:

Don't bite it, Wesley. Make love to it. Kiss it like you're worshiping a holy relic—reverence and awe. That's it, Cuckie. Sweet, open-mouth kisses. Use your tongue. Now put those fingers inside. That's what Mommy likes. That's a good boy.

She held my head against her, taking deep, slow breaths as I served.

"Does he taste good, Wormsie? I don't think I'll—oh, that's it, lick it right there. Goddamn, you're a worthless fuck, but you do know how to clean a girl up."

Her phone rang, and she held my head in place with her left hand as she answered with her right.

"What's the matter, Tony? Didn't get enough?"

A man's voice filtered through—words undistinguishable, lust unquenchable—*he was wooing my wife.*

"You wanna hear something naughty, Tone?"

She pushed my head down—harder than before. The voice mumbled its assent.

"You gotta promise you won't think I'm bad."

I dove in with my tongue.

"Guess what I'm doing right now?

She hit speaker and held the phone so I could hear.

His voice was deep, masculine, powerful—a real man's voice. "I hope you're playing with that sweet little pussy of yours."

"Nope."

"You better not be getting fucked—I'll beat your ass, Paula."

"Ughhh, gross."

"You don't like me beating that ass? I thought you liked that?"

She leaned over me, whispering her demands. "Keep it right there, Wormsie—real slow now."

"Are you talking to me?" he said, "You're pissing me off, girl."

"I'm with my roommate—*Mr. Wallace.* I'm talking to him."

"Oh, you're a dirty 'lil bitch. I asked if you were getting fucked, and you said no."

"Don't be silly. I'm not fucking him—that's practically impossible with his little dinky. He's on his knees, cleaning me up. Isn't that right,

Wormsie?"

I tried to answer—but she clenched my head with her legs.

"Goddamn, that's nasty, Baby. Let me talk to him."

"You're on speaker. Go ahead."

"You like the taste of my cum, fucker?"

Did I? Meaning, would I eat his spunk if it weren't pumped in her? No. I'm not gay. But with Paula holding me there, and me not trying to escape, I get how that might be hard for some of you to understand. I don't find men attractive. I find men, using my wife—pleasing her in ways I never could—undeniably sexy. And I love the power that women like her and Marcy hold over me. But I don't like dick. I'll suck it when I'm told to, but I'm basically straight.

"You get that little cunny all cleaned up and ready for tonight— Goddamn, I'm fucking rock solid, girl."

I swallowed a mouthful of his discarded seed.

"Bring that bitch to me, Wallace, and I'll show you how a real man fucks—got it?"

I mumbled my reply.

"Tony, I can't. I got that thing with Rachel tonight."

"Don't give me that shit, bitch. I want relief. I don't give a fuck what you got. You be here when my shift ends—9:30. Got it?"

"Yeah, I got it, Babe. I'll be there."

"Both of you. Bring 'ol dick-licker. He knows what I want."

As he hung up, she came—grinding her used vagina against me.

When she was through, she rose and walked back to the bedroom, leaving her cold coffee and semen-stained robe behind.

I washed her cup and tossed the robe in the laundry.

THERAPY

"I missed you last week, and if I'm not mistaken"—he flipped through a small leather notebook—"you weren't here the week before either."

"You needed a notebook to see that—really?"

"There you go—the proper use of sarcasm. How did that feel?"

"Good, I guess." I sat back, mulling it over. "Yeah, it felt alright, but…"

"Yes?"

"You're not going to beat me up for smarting off. You asked me to do it."

"You don't think you could employ sarcasm on the street? What about with Paula?"

I rolled my eyes.

"Right, maybe not."

His pipe wasn't lit, but he held it as if it were. He wore a heather-grey turtleneck over dark charcoal pants. No socks, slightly scuffed black loafers. He fancied himself a poet, but after hearing a selection of one of his works, I understood why he was still a therapist. I wasn't moved.

"Your mother says you're having difficulties at home. Any reason why she might think you need to return to treatment?"

"Seriously? She said that? Do I seem like a danger to myself or others?"

"No, not to my knowledge…"

He took another imaginary pull from his pipe, his wire-framed glasses catching the soft glow of the lamp.

"But, then again, I'm not with you twenty-four hours a day, am I?"

I sipped my water and stared out the window. The grounds were beautiful—rolling green hills stretching beneath towering pines.

"Terrence…"

"I prefer Dr. Waddell, please."

"Sorry. I'm an idiot." *He loves it when I dip beneath him.* "My mother, as you know, can be overbearing, and out of love, I try to appease her. I know I have it easier than most—a man of privilege, but that doesn't spare me from the day-to-day trials of normal men. I'm a shop owner—that alone brings its challenges. I've got a rebellious teenage daughter and a wife who didn't want to marry me. Under those conditions, I think I'm doing pretty well, don't you?"

"Yes." He made a chapel of his fingers. "Under those conditions, you are, *Wesley*."

He stressed my name, pointedly placing me below his title of doctor.

"And that was a well-articulated defense. I think you're quite capable of remaining… free. But one thing more, if I may… "

Ugh, this f'ing guy—always one more point he has to make. It's like he's trying to justify every cent my mother pays him. I wouldn't care if we sat here in silence. I wouldn't tell anyone. I'd just sit back, staring at that incredibly distressed toupee taped to his head.

"Wesley, as we all know, you struggle with perception and an inability to see the truth as it's laid out before you. I'd like to ask you a few questions. Simple answers—yes or no, when applicable. Are you ready?"

"Shoot."

"Your father—living or dead?"

"Living."

Yeah, I know what I told you earlier, but let's drop it. We'll discuss it later. I didn't think you needed every detail. Dead, not dead, what's the difference?

"You are the owner of a shop?"

"No, it's my mother's place." *He's such a f'ing prick.* "Can I ask a question?"

"Of course."

"Why are you doing this? Why are you trying to beat me down? Yeah, I missed a few sessions. I was busy. I couldn't get away."

He opened his notebook and started writing.

"Look, Terrence, I'm doing what she wants. You want to go to that hospital and visit that corpse she calls my father? He's been lying there for what, twenty-four years? Not saying a word, just breathing—assisted or expiring—an f'ing robot, doctor. That's what he is. I wish I had the balls to pull his cord."

He stopped writing and stared at me.

"I didn't mean that. It's just… my father was the only one who ever supported me. It's easier to think of him as dead."

He held his pipe to his mouth, pretended to inhale, then leaned back and closed his eyes.

"Terrence—Dr. Waddell—I know I need help. Your help. I promise I'll come every week. Just give me the chance to do this. Please."

He stood, crossed the space between us, and placed a hand on my shoulder, playing the father figure.

What an asshole. I'm ten years his senior, and if he ever sired a child, it'd be a miracle birth.

I sucked it up—took his grandiosity like I swallowed my mother's hate.

"I think you're doing just fine, Wesley. I'll tell Ethyl you should be allowed to continue as planned."

Jesus, I was glad to be out of there. As you've probably gathered, I'm not going because I think it helps me. It was, and is, my mother's idea—a condition of my parole, if you will. I follow a few of her dictates, pay her rent, kiss her withering ass, and get to live an "autonomous" life within the confines of a family trust.

As I left the building, I spotted the white public safety jeep cruising the east end drive—a Greenwood Hospital logo on its door and a highly functional officer with an intellectual disability behind the wheel. The hospital is essentially a sanitarium, but they also run programs for the disadvantaged and like to put higher-functioning patients to work. It gives the mongoloid a sense of purpose.

I was parked in the staff lot, and as expected, there was a pink courtesy note on my windshield. I park here every week, and every week I get the same notice. I don't think they realize it's the same car.

I pulled out of the gates and headed back to town. Paula wanted me home by five, and I wasn't about to disappoint her.

At the corner of Anderson Blvd. and Orange, there was a liquor store. I was thirsty and wanted a bottle for later, maybe a bag of chips. I parked out front. A few young toughs were hanging by the propane machine.

When I was younger, I wished I had a gang—a group of street-wise punks in black leather, with me at the head. Talking back, intimidating, using the girls and getting used. But I wasn't gang material. I was more of the lone figure on the outskirts, looking in.

"Hey, nice car, man. You got some change?"

The voice startled me—jumping out of my past and landing in today.

"No, I'm sorry." I tapped my wallet. "Only plastic."

"Bullshit, dude. What about your fucking ashtray?"

The second voice slammed me—*aggressive, sharp.*

"I know you ain't smoking in that piece of shit."

I turned to see who spoke, and as I did, I was tripped, hitting the pavement.

"Give me your fucking wallet, bitch."

I tried to get my legs under me, but before I could stand, a black motorcycle boot slammed into my stomach, and out came my breakfast.

"Watch your pant leg, Damone. Motherfucker's blowing."

In pain, through their laughter, I crawled toward the liquor store's door, my fingers frantically punching the pavement as if typing on a keyboard, trying to call up something, or someone to save me. *Click, click, click, click, click, click, click, click.*

No one came.

"Get his fucking paper, Dog."

I didn't know if I was being kicked, punched, or slapped—it was black flash after flash, sparkling lights of pain, and greed-driven hands unmercifully defiling my body—fighting their way into my pockets.

"Help me! Please! Help me!"

A voice reached from the wilderness.

"Get the fuck out of here! Little motherfuckers! I'll fucking do you, man!"

The beating stopped, the blows frozen midair. Rubber soles chirped on Slurpee-stained asphalt, jackets flew like evil wings—they were off.

I staggered to my feet and backed against the wall. The cashier from the market stood there, gripping a small wooden bat. I crowded behind him—hand on his belt for protection.

The boys fled on their bicycles, a trio of black-jacket riders flashing middle fingers as they tore down the boulevard.

"I've told those little fuckers to stay away from here. You okay?"

I nodded, still catching my breath, staying close. My hand slipped to my back pocket—*my wallet was still there*.

"That fucking afro kid lives right up the street. Do you wanna call someone?"

41

My voice steadied. "The police?"

"The police? They're fucking juveniles, man. Fucking cops won't do shit. Where you from, dude?"

Against his advice, I dialed the emergency number and made my report.

I waited in my car while the clerk brought me a small bottle of water.

It wasn't long before help arrived—not a black-and-white, but a golden-brown four door sedan, more civilian than official. A detective stepped out, followed by a young patrolman.

"Do you need medical attention?"

I hadn't thought about it. My hip was bruised, my slacks ruined—destined for the trash.

"No, I'm okay."

The detective sent the young officer to speak with the clerk while he stayed behind. He was big—6'2, maybe 6'3—built like he played football or something. Handsome too. *Yeah, that's a weird thing for a man to say, but not that weird if you're not all hung up.* He reminded me of one of those jock anti-perspirant commercials—Right Guard or...

"Is something funny?"

"No, I uh... "

"You just got robbed and assaulted. That's not something to laugh about. Is it?"

"I didn't get robbed."

I wiped the residue of my breakfast off my lips.

"We were called on a 211. You're saying they didn't take anything? Making a false police report is a crime. Is that what you did?"

"No, I uh.."

The young patrolman walked out of the mart, closing his notepad. "According to 'ol Hey-Zeus in there, he saw this one get out of the car, trip over the curb, and get laughed at by some kids. No robbery. More of a make-fun-of-the-sissy thing."

"They kicked me. They demanded my wallet. I was assaulted."

"The spic says one of those kids is thirteen—the others not much older."

The detective stood quite for a moment, almost as if replaying it in his head. Then he nodded at his young recruit.

"Kent, why don't you go get in the car? I'm gonna clean things up with uh… Mr. uh… "

"Wallace, Wesley Wallace."

He looked me over—not unkindly, but not exactly supportive either.

It felt like he was sizing me up. I wasn't lying—you know that. I was genuinely afraid for my life.

The detective pulled a card from his wallet.

"I don't think you made a false report, but you need to be real careful about that—especially these days. Hey-Zeus said they were kids—"

"I don't think that's his name."

"Yeah, whatever. In this neighborhood, I'm assuming they were colored?"

"They were African American, yes. At least the one boy was. The others might have been Puerto Rican—it's funny how the different Caribbean islands—"

"As I was saying, you're driving a late-model BMW into a neighborhood like this, and you're accusing a trio of young black kids of beating you and ripping off your wallet—except nothing's missing, and you probably just tripped. Do you know what they call a male Karen, Mr. Wallace?"

"I didn't know there was a term for that."

"I don't think there is yet, but if you don't watch your ass, they're going to be calling it a Wesley. Here's my card. Don't use it. And stay on the other side of Anderson. Over here? Nothing but lowlifes and lunatics."

Detective Anthony Acala turned and walked away.

DETECTIVE DICK

She was in the bedroom when I arrived.

"Oh my God, Paula—I was almost robbed."

She set her drink on the dresser. "Almost? That's not robbed, Wesley." She reached between her legs. "You're late. Do you see what's happening here?"

She did a slow pirouette. Her hair hung in long, perfect curls—her face unmade. She was wearing garters and an open-front bra that framed her breasts—seductively firm—accessible.

"Did you forget we were going out?" she said.

"I was robbed."

"*Almost.*"

"Look at me. They beat me."

She walked over and studied my face—lifted my chin with her hand—her long, perfectly manicured nails teasing the skin on my neck, lightly pinching.

"You don't look beat—scuffed up, maybe, but not beat." She shrugged her dismissal. "Pick out my dress, Wormsie."

Paula was the kind of woman who would get her nails done on the way to my funeral.

There were three dresses lying on the bed—two black, and one dark red. I'd seen her in the red one before—she was stunning in it. But the sheer black one, so revealing, was new. I picked it up. She smiled.

"I knew you'd go there."

She pulled it over her head. It was basically like she'd clothed herself in a shadow; the fabric did nothing to conceal.

"I'm going to need a coat, Worm—or that black-and-white robe. We'd get arrested if I went like this."

I sat down on a cushioned stool and watched as she flitted about—smoothing and caressing herself, applying her makeup. *Tony was a lucky man—me too. I may not be getting what he's getting, but I'd get a taste of it.*

She smelled like sex should—wild and close, like a flesh-field of summer flowers and warm, spiced mornings.

"Go get a shower, Wormsie. I'll lay out your things."

She rode in the back—played with herself as I drove. I was wearing one of my sweat suits—the green Adidas with yellow stitching. I was surprised when I saw it on the bed and questioned her choice.

"He's got a big cock, Wormsie—you're gonna be working out."

She could be such a bitch.

I'll admit, I was turned on as we drove. I was instructed not to touch myself, but it was difficult. I'd seen her screw on film—begging to be filled, violated, used. But tonight, I was to be in the room—watching, hopefully participating....

"You missed the fucking turn off, you idiot."

She sat up quick, glanced over my seat, and checked my hands—two and ten, both on the wheel, not on my wand.

"You just cost us ten minutes. You're not rubbing that little weenie, are you?"

"No. You told me not to."

"Damn right, I did."

She leaned back and got on her phone—speaker engaged. It went to voicemail. She hung up and dialed again. This time, he answered.

"Pretty little Paula. I was just gonna call you."

"Don't get mad, Tony— "

"Mad? Why? You better be on your way."

"We are—just a little late."

"He's with you?"

"He's driving."

"That a girl. I got held up a minute, so I ain't tripping. There's a carport behind my place—park in C-22 and go upstairs. In the pot next to the door, there's a key. Go on in, make yourself at home. I'll be there in a bit."

"You keep a key by the door? Aren't you worried about intruders?"

"Baby, I live for the day someone breaks into my place—hopefully, when I'm lying in bed—fully armed."

He was laughing as I took the exit, made a U-turn, and went south.

"Can your hubby hear me?"

"Hang on a minute, Babe."

She held the phone to my ear.

"Go ahead. He's listening."

"Hey, boy?"

His voice sounded familiar—where the hell did I know it from?

"Yes?"

"I want you to get her ready—I want that pussy clean and that asshole real wet. Open her up."

"Yes, sir."

"Oh, you've done this before?"

"No, sir. I've never prepared her."

"Paula?"

"I'm here. I can hear you. He's full of shit. He's never seen me get fucked, but he got me ready—remember that young man at the shop, Wormsie? The one with the big dick?"

I remembered. I went down on Paula while he watched. Then I was kicked out of the room so he could screw her in private.

Tony didn't dig my forgetfulness.

"Hit him for me."

"What?"

"You heard me, Baby. I want you to slap his face."

I didn't have time to defend myself. She hit hard, the flat-hand sting jerking my head violently to the left. I swerved into the lane next to us— *thankfully unoccupied.*

"I don't like liars, bitch. We're gonna have to break you of that."

He said more, but I couldn't focus—goddamn, she hit hard. I was still seeing stars, fighting to hold the wheel straight. I knew I deserved it—but there's a place for punishment, and 70 mph on the cross-town parkway isn't it. It stung until we reached his place.

I was on my knees when he walked in. Paula was bent over in front of me. I had her ass spread, my tongue licking and darting inside of her.

I love the taste of her, although I think it's better when she isn't as fresh as she is tonight.

He stood over me and laughed. "Oh no, there's been a robbery."

I knew that voice was familiar. It was Tony, Detective Anthony Acala.

She kissed him, his hands sliding down—palming her ass, teasing her before reaching between her legs. Her lips pulled his fingers in as he worked.

"Don't let me stop you, Baby," he said—"carry on." He pulled away from her. "I'm gonna pour myself a drink."

She turned around and pushed her rump against my face. I continued to serve.

I could hear the cupboard open, the refrigerator, the cubes of ice bouncing off each other as they fell into the glass, and the heavy pour of the alcohol. *I'd assume he was a single malt drinker, but I wouldn't have been surprised if it was bourbon—maybe he wasn't as tough as he looked.*

"How you doing there, Wesley? I'm sure glad you didn't get smoked today."

Paula wiggled against me. "You know each other?"

"Not as well as we're going to, but I came to the rescue of that little ass-eating damsel of yours. He was assailed by a gang of angry negroes—or should I say, *Caribbeans*. Ha!"

He sat down on an armless chair near the sofa and placed his keys on the TV. Nearby, sat a large gold frame—a family photo: Tony, his wife, two kids. *I wonder where they are.*

"Come on, Baby." He spread his arms—tan, muscular. "Let me see you."

Paula walked over and stood before him. From where I knelt, she was beautiful—a pet stepped out of a magazine. He looked her over for a minute, then pushed her aside.

"Get over here, pussy. Take my shoes off."

I crawled to where he sat. He wore a pair of black trainers—cop shoes. *Cheap, in my opinion, but I guess if you need a little more tread—not wanting to slip in the muck of a decomposing body—they'll do.*

"Hold up, punk. I'm gonna need you to give 'em a little kiss first."

He put his arm around Paula's waist and pulled her close. She leaned down and nuzzled his cheek. I lifted his right leg and held the sole of his foot facing me. I leaned forward.

"Hold up."

I looked at him. It was the first time our eyes met. Neither one of us turned away until he raised his glass—*oh, God. You've got to be kidding. The vessel I'd heard ice fall into was a tumbler, and the alcohol was some sort of red wine. Who's the faggot now, bitch?*

"Paula, get Daddy that big cigar over there. I want to enjoy this." He looked back at me. "Okay, Wesley. She says you're real good with that tongue. I want a nice long lick from heel to toe."

Things are never as bad as you think—imaginations run wild, conjuring the worst. People get it in their heads that licking the bottom of a shoe would be inch after long inch of bright, vibrant disgust, but it's not. After the first lick, it's the same dull, dirty taste all the way across. Bon appétit.

When I lifted his left leg, I felt the bulge.

"Hold up, little man."

He put his foot on the floor and pulled up his pant leg. Strapped below a large, muscled calf, on the inside edge of his leg, was a black leather holster and, what I was soon to learn, was a snub-nose .38 special.

He unfastened it and placed the gun on the floor beside him.

"Fuck that shoe-licking, punk—take 'em off, and pull down my pants."

He accommodated me by lifting his ass.

"Now fold 'em real nice and set 'em on that table."

I got up and did as he asked—folded his slacks and set them neat. When I turned back, Paula was sitting on his leg, rubbing his crotch and kissing him. He broke it off, and pushed her away.

"Come get these *chonies* now."

I walked over and leaned down. He kicked me in the stomach—a hard, flat-footed push that sent me tumbling.

"Nobody told you to stand over me. Stop fucking crying and crawl up between my legs."

I wasn't crying—I was trying to breathe. That kick floored me, and I couldn't get my wind.

"Come on. Do it. We don't got all night, guy."

I crawled between his legs, using his muscled thighs as support.

If I thought he looked like a commercial actor before, his BVD-covered cock could've been the lobby poster for a Johnny Wad film.

I reached for his waistband and tugged.

"Put your fucking face down on it, punk. I want that fucker to bang your pride when he's sprung."

I leaned down. He smelled like sweat, piss, and ass. He was dirty, unshowered after work.

"Get your fucking face on it, boy."

He shoved my face into his crotch, rubbing his cotton-covered cock against me.

"Pull 'em down now—real slow, I wanna watch that big 'ol head pop out."

I inched his briefs down until the shaft appeared. He was ridiculously thick—like the proverbial child's forearm in his pants. When the head came free, it hit me below the chin, leaving a trail of precum across my face as he rose.

He kicked me to the side.

"Get the fuck out of there."

He pulled Paula between his legs and forced her to her knees. She held his cock with both hands and dropped her mouth over the head. She was loud—slurping and moaning, making no secret of the cock-hungry slut she was.

I was forgotten.

She pleasured him with her mouth, then climbed onto his lap, guiding his cock. I watched as the head fought its way inside her lips. After an inch or two of hard going, her body surrendered and swallowed him to the balls—ten inches, thick-as-an-arm, stuffed inside her box.

As she rode him, I stared at his gun.

It looked like it'd flatter my hand.

I saw myself standing—legs slightly spread, intimidating—much taller than I am, fully erect. A tailored black wool suit, expensive Italian loafers on my feet, and that magnanimous prick, Dr. Waddell—why the fuck did I just think of him? Oh, well, might as well fantasy-shoot him as anyone else—and Dr. Waddell, on his knees before me, begging for his life: please, please, please! Sorry, bud. Business is business. Bang!

Paula was getting loud. His hands gripped her waist—squeezing, leaving dark finger marks on her flesh. He pushed her down on his cock, burying it to the hilt. I watched as his balls contracted and his thick pipe pumped her full of cum.

This is what I was waiting for.

I assumed my position—on my knees, lustful, begging.

He lifted her off his tool—the head disengaged, and the length fell across his thigh. She turned to me.

"Come get it, Wormsie."

"What are you doing, girl?"

He sat up, his tone sharp.

"He's gonna clean me."

"Like fuck if he is—what'd he do for that?"

He shoved her aside and stood over me. "You wanna taste that pussy, Wesley? Is that what you want?"

He was a monster compared to me—the epitome of the Italian male, with dark curly hair and a long thick scar snaking across his abdomen.

He held his cock in his hand, dripping with my wife's desire and his cum.

I looked up, my eyes pleading.

"Open that mouth, motherfucker. I'm gonna let you taste it."

He fed me as I knelt on the rug—his cock swelling again as I sucked.

I could taste Paula on him, but when he came, she was washed down my throat and only he remained.

THE REALTOR

They were looking for something—something hidden, poisonous, deadly.

My mother's voice echoed from somewhere below.

"Don't drink it, Wesley. Don't drink it."

She slapped a glass from my hand. It cartwheeled across the table and landed in Rachel's lap.

"No es mota, pendejo—es veneno."

"Ay, cabron! Ha!"

I was dreaming in Spanish. Shit. I don't even speak Spanish. What the hell were they talking about? There was a gang of them—machetes, Rachel, the yard? Jesus…

It took me a minute to shake it off—you know those dreams, the did-that-really-happen thing—story of my life, huh?

I'd slept on the couch—one thin blanket, and a small floral throw pillow—the window at my back. We have six bedrooms—four of them unused—but Paula likes me where she can keep an eye on me. Besides, she says, it's weird when couples have two rooms. So, that's where I was.

I'm normally up early, but last night took more out of me than I thought.

Paula was still asleep. She lay in the middle of the bed—surrounded by a white fortress of pillows, a puffed purple satin mask over her eyes.

I could still taste him.

When I got home and brushed my teeth, I had a flash of concern about the cleanliness of his member. I don't think he was infected with anything—you never know, though. I knew a man who had herpes since he was thirteen—said he got it from his sister. I'll have to ask Paula where she met him.

I put on my sweatpants—the same as last night—but when I grabbed the top, semen stains ran down the bib. I doubt anyone would've known what they were, but...

"Look, mommy, that man has a huge load blasted on his jacket."

No thanks. I'll wear something else.

God-swab, is that what I am now—a cum-gobbler? The kind of man who butters up the bread and licks the corn clean.

I didn't like it.

Having Paula boss me around was one thing—I get off on that kind of play—but having that fat-dicked prick holding my reins wasn't cool in any way. I'm only a pretend bitch.

Then why'd you do it, Wesley? Why'd you go down on him?

Who knows? I guess I've done plenty of things I didn't feel good about in the morning—arguments with people who probably shouldn't get stressed out when they've got a heart condition, or feeding something dangerous to someone without knowing it's poison.

I think I'll sit out next time. She can go do her thing, but I'll wait here. Hell, I'll even drive her if she wants, but I don't wanna do that again.

I'm gonna look up 'cuck.' Pretty sure I've got the definition skewed.

"Goddamn it, Pedro! You gotta move that wood. Where the fuck's Bruno?"

What the heck? There *were* voices in the yard.

I threw on a t-shirt and house shoes. It was only 7:30, but it felt later.

I walked downstairs. The backyard door was open, and a pot of coffee was simmering on the counter.

I wasn't aware of anything going on this morning. Paula was lights out, and Rachel was at a friend's—*she'd been doing that a lot more often lately.*

I slammed hard into the bathroom door—it was closed a second ago.

An overweight Mexican man in blue jeans and a stained Padres shirt walked out of my bathroom. His work boots were filthy—leaving small clumps of dirt on the freshly mopped tiles. He was buttoning his pants.

"Tienes un problema en el baño, eh."

"Excuse me! Who are you?"

I had no idea what the heck he was saying, but if it had anything to do with that foul odor trailing him from the toilet, I could only imagine.

"Bruno!" a man's voice called from outside. "Where the hell are you—oh, there you are. How's it going, Wes?"

Bradberry stepped into my kitchen—perfectly coiffed hair, powder-blue suit, white collared shirt unbuttoned just low enough to show the gold chain around his neck, and no tie. He had the air of someone whose ass I'd love to kick.

"Jesus Christ, Wes—smells like you shit your pants in here."

The man I assumed was Bruno brushed by me and headed to the backyard. Bradberry's voice chased him outside.

"Get those goddamn palms cut down so we can take out that hedge and open up that rear area. *Comprende?*"

I needed coffee—and a valium.

"I don't think he speaks English. What are you doing here, Bradberry? Who let you in?"

He waved a trio of keys on a ring—*I'd seen them before: my house, the pool house, our garage.*

"I don't get a hello?" He set down my favorite coffee cup and held out his sun-tanned hand. "Your mother set me up. I'm gonna help her clean this place up and put it on the market."

"What the hell are you talking about? This is my home."

"How long's it been since you fired up that pool? You sure let this place go, huh?"

"The pool? It's empty."

He poured himself a warm-up. "You want a cup of this, Wes?"

"It's Wesley, and I don't understand. How did you get those keys? Who told you to do this?"

He looked at me like I was slow, incapable of comprehending simple English.

"I think you should call your mother, Sport. Want me to dial it?"

"No! I want you to get the—"

"Ohh, there she is—"

My wife walked into the room, her robe loosely wrapped, hair hanging in that just-got-fucked style she favors.

"Goddamn, girl. If I knew you were part of the deal, I'd have come here years ago."

"Wesley, why didn't you tell me we had company?"

Bradberry laughed. "I don't think little Wes here knows what's happening."

Paula shot me a dismissive glance—"I'm not surprised."

They both laughed.

He hugged her, his hands blatantly rubbing her hips before he let go.

"Can I get you anything, Mr. Bradberry?"

"No, I'm doing good, darling—call me Richard, or Big Dick if you're in that kind of mood. I got my boys out back. We'll get that yard straightened out and bring in someone to fix the pool—you know you've got poisonous plants out there. A frigging death trap for the unawares."

He smiled at me.

What the hell did my mother tell him?

Paula let her fingers graze down his arm. "We're lucky to have someone like you on it."

"I'm not on it yet, Babe, but I will be."

Paula laughed and poured herself a cup of coffee, her robe slipping off one shoulder.

If I didn't know better, I'd think they were lovers.

"Does someone want to tell me what's going on?"

"Well, Wes, if someone had been doing their due around here, I'd be rubbing suntan lotion on this beautiful wife of yours, and you'd be whipping us up a couple of cocktails. But as it is… you're gonna call your mommy, and I'm gonna make sure my boys aren't sleeping on the job."

He gave Paula a pat on the ass and poked his head into the bathroom.

"Whooof. You better grab a plunger and clean up your mess, Wesley—that's a big turd for a little body."

"Mom, what are you doing? I live here."

"Richard thinks it's better to sell that place now—while the market's good—and set you up on the east end. That way, if you had to return to Greenwood, Paula and Rachel would be close."

"The east end? Are you talking about the old Martin place? Come on, Mom. It's a dump."

"We'll throw a coat of paint on it, and you can buy some new carpet—maybe then you'll respect it. And speaking of that, does it feel good to take advantage of me?"

Don't do it, Wesley. Don't say anything.

"Does it? Answer me."

"I don't think I'm taking advantage of you."

"Then explain the yard. Richard said the pool's going to take a few thousand to make right, and the backyard looks like a jungle. He called it nothing but spider nests, cigar butts, and a carpet of broken whiskey bottles—cheap whiskey. You've been drinking again?"

"I wasn't aware that Mr. Bradberry could be so verbose."

"What'd you say? Are you smarting me?"

"No, ma'am."

"You know, Dr. Waddell has been known to be off on his recommendations."

She hung up.

I was late for work.

I left Paula under the watchful eyes of Bruno, Pedro, and Big Dick—then took off.

The cigars, I'll admit to—but a bottle or two doesn't make a carpet of broken glass. Bradberry was pumping this fire for all it's worth. If he wasn't around, she wouldn't be doing this.

THE NEW BOSS

I arrived before Marcy. The store was in good shape. Sure, she was putting the screws to me, but she was keeping up with her work. This could've turned into a no-work-just-pay deal, but it hadn't... *yet.*

Maybe I dodged a bullet.

I made myself a cup of coffee and sat on the ottoman beneath the hat wall.

Fucking Waddell. I used to have feelings. Sure, things got out of hand sometimes—depression ain't fun. The manic side was, but you can't always stay there can you? I get it—the swings weren't right. But it's also not right to go through everything feeling nothing.

Maybe that's why I do what I do.

He's pushed the edge so far with the Lexapro, the Elavil, and the fucking Zyprexa that I don't even begin to feel anything until I've blown past where feelings should've stopped. Seriously, it's like I'd have to kill myself to hurt.

I pinched my forearm, squeezing hard enough to make my eyes sting.

I tried to align each tear to an incident in my life, but they weren't tied to anything. The tears were from physical pain. The incidents? Just events—nothing with the emotional catalyst to inflame me.

"What're you doing, Boss Man?"

Marcy stood over me. I let go of my forearm and looked up at her, my eyes rimmed with tears. Her face softened.

"I'm not gonna call the cops, Wesley. You can stop worrying."

"I don't care if you do." My voice was flat, detached from emotion. "I'm not upset about that."

Her eyes dropped to my arm—red, swollen, bruised.

"What the fuck are you doing?"

I stared at her without reply.

"Hey, retard. What the fuck's wrong with you?"

"They're selling my house. My mother wants me to go back to the hospital, and my wife made me suck some cop's dick."

I laughed as I said it, and she joined me—both of us caught in the absurdity of my complaints.

"You're fucking crazy, Wesley. I bought you a present."

"With my money?"

"Don't trip. It wasn't that expensive. Besides, you're gonna love it."

I stood up, a moment away from hugging her, but then she turned away.

As I walked toward my office, she tripped me, and I fell into a rack of dresses.

"Playtime's over dickless—it's back to work."

I'd taken out an ad in the local rag, and the turnout was better than expected. I was thinking about Charles. He hated work. He'd refer to my customers as bitches and pigs—I never would. Still, it can be trying being of service to a hard-to-please consumer. I know they just want to be heard, but I'd prefer they used a less demanding, quieter tone when they expressed their needs.

Marcy was wonderful. Some women aren't comfortable with a pretty young girl waiting on them, but Marcy had something about her that spoke more of daughter than rival.

We even had time to play—a knuckle in my back, a slap to my

balls—and in the afternoon, a few hours before closing, she told me the changing room needed attendance.

The shop was empty, so I strolled to the back and found a pair of what I hoped were Marcy's panties sitting on the settee. I glanced over my shoulder—the curtain had closed behind me.

I held them to my nose—slightly moist, lightly stained. I inhaled the scent—a young girl's musk—excellent. I slid my hand down my pants and squeezed my balls. I'm not sure of the mechanics, but when I cover my manhood with my hand, encompassing all of me as best I can, I can get off just by repeatedly squeezing my—

The curtain flew aside. Marcy barged in.

"What the fuck are you doing? Are those my panties?"

I tried to pull my hand from my pants, but it got caught in the waistband. She lunged at me—grabbing my arms and shoving me against the large changing room mirror. Her knee slammed into my crotch.

"I thought we were doing better, Wesley. I was willing to give you a second chance."

Her breath smelled like cigarettes and spearmint gum. She ground her knee into me, pressing hard.

"Marcy, I'm—"

"Sorry? Is that what you were about to say?"

"I thought we were—"

"We're nothing—you don't fucking get it, do you? You're a creep, and I'm a princess."

She grabbed my hair, one hand on each side of my head.

"Do you jerk off, Wesley? Is that what you were doing?"

"I squeeze myself."

"Can you cum?"

"Yes, I uh…"

"Do it. Now. Cum for me."

I squeezed my cock as she held me—*I wouldn't last long.*"

"Open wide, asshole."

I opened my mouth. She spit in it. Pulled me closer—almost close enough to kiss—and spit again. Then again.

"You better cum quick, pretty boy, or you're gonna drown in my spit."

The bells on the front door rang—a customer.

Instantly, she released my hair and smoothed herself. For a moment, I thought she wanted us to stay silent—two kids caught making out by our parents. Then something shifted. Her eyes filled with tears, and she pointed to the couch. I was to sit and wait.

She walked out to greet the customer.

"Good afternoon, ma'am. I'm sorry for the delay—"

"Are you okay, dear?"

"Yes, I apologize. I was on the phone—this isn't very professional."

What the fuck is she doing—crying, in front of a customer?

"It's okay. I'm willing to listen."

"I shouldn't be doing this."

"You're goddamn right you shouldn't.

"Sweetheart, if two gals can't help each other out, who can? What's the matter?"

"I'm not supposed to use the phone at work—not for personal business—but of course, I did, and now this."

"Mr. Wallace yelled at you for using the phone? I could speak to him."

That voice—it sounds like Mrs. McManus, the youth counselor. Oh my God. Where's Marcy going with this? That crazy little bitch.

"No, never. Mr. Wallace is almost too kind. It was my boyfriend."

"Oh, young love. I remember my first crush. How old are you, sweetheart—sixteen?"

"I turned seventeen in December, but he's not my first. He's mad at me because I acted like a spoiled brat."

Oh, Christ. She's out of her mind....

"We went to dinner for his birthday, and then he got us a hotel."

"A hotel? Sweetheart, I don't want to sound like a prude, but some things, especially a woman's body, should be saved for marriage and—"

"He's already married."

Okay, Wesley, you gotta make a move here—walk out. I can't. Walk out! I can't! She'll fucking kill me.

"What?"

"Yeah, that's why we have to use a hotel. If his wife, or my father, caught us together, we'd be dead."

"I don't understand, darling. He's married and seeing you on the side? How old is your boyfriend?"

"He's fifty-six. It was his birthday last night. His wife thought he was out of town, but he was here with me. Isn't that romantic?"

"No… it's not. It's called adultery, dear. You must know that."

"That's what I said when we started sleeping together, but he told me girls my age shouldn't think like that. He said man wasn't meant to be with one woman—and women, weren't meant to be with one man. That's how the fight started. I wanted to be alone with my Carson on his birthday, but when we got to the hotel, two of his drunken bar buddies were naked and waiting for us."

Oh, fuck. I'll tell people she was ill… off her meds, diabetic.

"I didn't like it—why can't I be as open-minded as he is? I did everything they wanted, but I guess I could've been more willing. More appreciative."

The conversation had become one-sided. I assumed Mrs. McManus was still listening—but who knows.

"Do you think I was wrong to be so selfish?"

"I'm not sure what to think."

"That's how I feel. Maybe he's right, but sometimes I still think a girl should be a one-man woman—not that it doesn't feel good to be the center of three men's attention, to be his 'little hole'—that's what he likes to call me. Cute huh? But I do sometimes feel like a hoochie girl.

I guess that's normal, right?"

"Dear, I don't think any of this is normal, and I'm sorry I asked. If I were you, I'd call the police or a therapist."

I heard the bells sing at the front door. Mrs. McManus was gone—probably for good. Marcy joined me.

"Did you like that, Wesley?"

"You're out of your mind."

"You didn't like it? I thought you'd get off on that "little hole" thing. You should've seen her face—looked like she swallowed a turd when I dropped that bomb. Ha!"

"She's the youth director at the church. My wife and daughter are parishioners."

"Fuck her and those parishioners."

"Marcy!"

"And fuck that church. I did that Bible shit—I lived it."

"What are you talking about?"

"Look at my eye—do I look like I play tennis. My father did this to me. I took a page out of his Bible, and I got the shit beaten out of me."

She grabbed her panties from my hand and left the room. I followed her out but gave her space.

At 5:00, I locked the front door.

"What are you doing?" She asked.

"I was thinking we had a good day—it's been quiet for an hour, so let's lock up and go home."

"My mom's not coming until six."

"You can call her, have her come early, or I could drop you off. I was gonna sit and have a glass of wine, but I can wait until I get home."

"Could I join you?"

"With the wine?"

I don't know why that worried me—situational ethics. I can look at her little pussy, swallow her piss, but somehow it's wrong to enjoy a nice glass of pinot with her? Ridiculous.

"Yeah, I'd love that."

Maybe the vino would loosen her up...

OLD TIME RELIGION

"Have you ever read the Bible, Wesley?"

I was distracted, getting off on the way she sat before me, sipping her wine, twirling her hair, and occasionally brushing her fingers along the soft, clean lines of her neck. My thoughts wandered to that older boyfriend and his drunken friends. I wouldn't have minded being part of that soiree.

"Are you listening?"

"Yeah, I'm a big fan."

She laughed. "I was, too—until I took it a bit too literally, and it cost me this." She touched the scar on her brow. "—and my grandfather."

She took another drink—*I loved the way her lips caressed the rim of that glass, the way the curve distorted them. I wanted to taste her.*

"I'm trying to tell you about a life-changing event, and you're being a creep."

She pulled me out of my seat, turned our chairs back-to-back, and pushed me down. She sat behind me. "Face forward, Wesley."

If I leaned back, I could smell her hair—a light, innocent scent slightly mixed with—

"Wesley, I'm not fucking with you. I ain't playing."

"How do I know?"

"You watch that tone, boy."

I could feel her bristling behind me—Old Ambrose raising his belt.

"I'm sorry, Miss Marcy, it's just that... you like to tease. It's hard to know when you're fooling around—we need a code word."

"How 'bout "faggot"? If you ever suggest a fucking safe word again, I'll clip your balls. Now shut up. My mother's gonna be here soon."

She slid back—just a few inches of distance between us.

"You know she watches me like a hawk, right?"

"Well, I know she, uh—"

"Wesley!"

"Sorry... jeez."

"I'm almost never out of her sight. I don't know why she thinks me working here is okay, but I'm guessing it has something to do with your sexuality—and the fact that you own a women's shoe store."

"My sexuality? Your mother doesn't know a thing about me."

"Only what I tell her. She believes you're a repentant homosexual—relieved of your desires, found God's path, and now attempting to live righteously."

"Oh."

"Yeah. Now shut up."

I closed my eyes—*focus, focus, focus.*

"I was a troubled kid—mentally ill. My depressive episodes, suicide attempts, and manic outbursts terrified my parents. They thought I was possessed, driven by the manipulations of the devil."

Possession? Give me a break. I thought she was going somewhere with this—a bond forming between us. I exhaled hard.

She threw her head back and cracked me—skull against skull.

"Fuck, Marcy! Goddamn it!"

"I told you to keep your fucking mouth shut."

"I was breathing—shit." I rubbed my head. "I think I'm bleeding."

"You know what you were doing. Bleed quiet."

I did.

She returned to the story.

My head was killing me.

"Do you know that church on the outskirts of the yards? It's on the hill above the 58."

I knew the place, but I was afraid to answer. Their congregation was infamous for picketing funerals, clinics, and Halloween parades.

"My parents had Father Hezekiah pray over me—an exorcism of sorts—and he proclaimed me healed.

"They were thrilled. I promised to attend youth service programs and devote myself as a thank-you for my deliverance. I dove into the Good Book with zeal, starting at Genesis and working my way through. I was thirteen years old.

"My grandfather on my mother's side didn't believe as we did. He was a sinner—an outcast, shunned by our family. But when my parents needed him, they forgave him. He was my sitter on the nights they attended the adult program—I guess their desire to worship trumped his evils.

"I liked the way he smelled—that sharp old-man cologne, the Bay Rum. I'm not sure why, but I felt sorry for him. His hands trembled slightly—a side effect, I later learned, of going without liquor.

"I'd heard talk about his alcoholism, and my mother always threw the same line at my father when he went to retrieve him. 'Not a drop, Archie. Not one drop.'

"The Church of the Holy Word doesn't prohibit alcohol, gambling, or any of the lesser vices. They frown on excess, assuming a member in good standing—reborn in the spirit—would forsake those things on their own merit.

"My father kept a bottle in our cupboard—a fifth of Old Grandad, which I thought amusing since they hid it whenever my grandfather arrived. But I knew where it was.

"One night, after my parents had gone, my grandfather and I were on the couch, cuddled close and watching a teen movie. I could feel him shaking, and I felt bad for him. I excused myself—said I needed a bathroom break—and retrieved the bottle from my parents' room.

"I poured my plastic tumbler half-way full and I handed it to him.

"Have you ever seen an alcoholic drink, Wesley?"

"Yeah. I've seen those guys at the…"

"I'm talking about the ones who shake and hurt, who live disconnected from that force that flows through the world. I'm talking about the ones who, when they take a drink, they change—they light up and become whole.

"I gave my grandfather that drink, and instantly the shaking stopped. His frail old hands grew strong, and his youth—vitality, hope, and lust—returned. He pounded that glass—a vessel four inches full—in one breath, maybe two.

"And then he looked at me as if I were the last drop in the last bottle on earth. He put his arms around me, lifted me onto his lap, and cradled me. He buried his head against me and lightly kissed my neck. I had never been held so close or felt so loved.

"When he put his hand between my legs, I indulged him. He rubbed my crotch as he kissed me, pulling my underwear to the side. Then he placed his finger in my mouth, asked me to suck it—to get it wet—and slid it along my cunt.

"When I pushed against him, it entered me. There was pain, but it was good. I felt as if I had purpose and meaning—like my submission was God-inspired.

"He rolled me over and pushed me back on the couch. As he looked at me and pulled my panties off, I saw his eyes—the old man was gone. Whoever he was, or whatever he had become, had taken over.

"He got on his knees, spread my legs, and held them open. He bent down, fed on my innocence, my youth, and I let him—with pleasure.

"When he stood up and removed his pants, I felt a moment of trepidation. Fear. I had plied my grandfather with liquor. Would I be damned?

"Genesis 19:31-35. Come, let us make our father drunk with wine, and we will lie with him."

"I was thirteen years old, Wesley. A little girl.

"My grandfather was a powerful man. He leaned over me and placed the head of his cock at my entrance, nestled within my lips. He lifted my legs and pressed forward—a great, powerful stroke that filled me beyond comfort. I lost my breath, and with his mouth over mine, I became lightheaded.

"His thrusts were relentless and steady, untouched by his age. When he came, it felt as if he had given the last of himself. He lay still in my arms—gone."

"What?"

"My grandfather died when he came—a heart attack. He was lying on me when my parents entered the room. I didn't know he passed—neither did my mother. She screamed, grabbed him by the hair, and that's when she realized he was dead.

"My father dragged him off me—my grandfather's semi-clothed body collapsing to the floor—and I lay there with my legs spread, the remnants of his act slipping from me like a tearful goodbye.

"I stood without shame, stared my father in the eyes, and that's when he hit me. His blow sent me reeling, and as I fell, the edge of the coffee table split my brow.

"My mother and father cleaned my grandfather's body with a wet towel, they dried and dressed him, leaving him lying on the floor. My mother drove me to the hospital while my father waited for the police.

"He was an old man—no inquiry would be made. My mother blamed herself for what happened. I think it might have happened to her too—maybe that's why he didn't live with us. My father blamed me. It was a year or two before we spoke."

"I knew there was something wrong when you put that—"

"Are you kidding me, Wesley? Just sit with that a minute. I don't need your fucking thoughts."

She was right—if it was true, it was horrifying. I felt awful.

She took out her phone and called her mother.

"Mom, I'm off early. Do you think you could—oh, okay, great. I'll be out back."

She returned her chair to the table and popped a piece of gum in her mouth.

"I bought you a present the other day, but I don't think you're ready for it. If I come in tomorrow, maybe you can try it on. If I don't, don't call me, don't pursue me, and don't try to contact me in any way. I still have those bathroom videos, and I have no trouble using them against someone who has neither the character nor the class to respect my wishes. Later, asshole."

She was gone.

Goddamn it. I'd prefer punishment over rejection.

What are you supposed to do when someone tells you a story like that? I was trying to be sympathetic, but I didn't even know if she was telling the truth. Something had to have happened—she's crazier than shit—but sleeping with her grandfather, beaten by her dad, possessed? It sounded like an X-rated soap opera.

I'm gonna be honest with you, though—that little girl makes me forget my troubles. She's given me a reason to be—not that I was thinking of dying. Don't go running off to my mother and Dr. Waddell, telling them I'm a danger to myself. But that line of hers—purpose and meaning—that's exactly how I feel. She's given me a reason to live.

I was in no hurry to go home.

I wanted to see Charles. I sat at my desk and began a new page.

Click, click, click—punch. Click, click, click—punch....

I was in the market the other day, grabbing a couple things—a bottle of Kessler, two Cokes, and one of those kid's sandwich kits—you know, the kind good mothers used to give their boys after school. I know they ain't for adults, but they're tasty.

I was in line, waiting to pay, when a small disturbance broke out—

not the lady with the bottle of vodka and twenty cans of cat food. It was two young punks in front of her—a pair of low-life assholes making fun of the box-girl. The fucking checker didn't have the balls to say anything, and the old cunt manager was pretending to look the other way—fucking coward.

I intervened.

"Hey boys. Why don't you grab your things and hit the road."

For some reason, my comment was amusing. I realize I'm not the best at interpersonal relationships, but I thought my communication skills were on point.

"Get this, man. Home-squeeze doesn't like us fucking with his girlfriend."

The kid who said this could've used a toothbrush, and an eraser to remove the tattoos from his face.

His partner joined the party. "Is that the problem, Mr.? Is that thing yours?"

The problem—that's interesting—where is it?

First the problem was them, getting their kicks by teasing a box-girl who was, as we used to say in school, slow or retarded. Then the problem shifted to the two boys themselves—their inability to perceive a threat. They thought I was less than dangerous—just a normal man in line with his sandwich kit, a bottle of booze, and a couple of cokes.

And then as if that wasn't enough, the problem jumped to me. I was posturing—exhibiting bravado in front of an attractive woman I'd taken a physical interest in. If I didn't play this straight—weak, vulnerable to my attackers—I'd miss my chance to get my hands dirty and my cock wet.

"Look, guys, I'm sorry for speaking up. It's none of my business."

"You're fucking right it ain't your business."

The one without the tattooed face was calling the shots.

"But if you'd like to take it outside, we could get you involved."

Sometimes I really get off on myself. I'm a problem solver. One fucking line, and they stopped bothering my girl-to-be and offered themselves to me instead.

I hung my head as they paid.

When it was my turn, the checker slighted me—flipped me that here-comes-the-bitch glance. A look that said I was nothing but a punk.

Fuck her.

The cowardly manager poked his head in to check on his "special" employee—Debbie.

Wow. That name tag hung on a piece of female art that belonged in a museum, not standing in a dirty apron behind a bitch checker in a cut-rate supermarket—hottie on aisle one.

I'd never been attracted to a retarded chick before—I'm not even sure it's legal—but I dug her eyes, man. You ever notice how those slow broads have that exotic look on their faces? It's the slant, dude—that angle of the eyes that turns toward heaven.

Blonde, too. Bit of curl in her hair. Her clothes were shit—Jumbo Mart brand, but maybe she just didn't have anybody to get her something nice.

I checked her left hand—unadorned pudgy little fingers, no ring. Freckles on her wrists. She was single.

I could see the two low-life's through the front window of the market. Another young hood had joined them—friendly, chatting it up, probably having a laugh at my expense. Maybe they were waiting for me.

When Debbie bagged my groceries, I caught her eye—smiled, and then quickly looked away. The shy boy routine. I wasn't sure if she had the mental capabilities to pick up on it, but I guess God created man and woman with an innate mating sense, because when I looked back, she was touching her hair—a sure sign of physical attraction.

The boys braced me as I came out of the store. I tried to step around them, but they blocked my path.

"You wanna play, tough guy?"

"I just want to go to my car—I'm sorry about mouthing off."

"Not yet, you ain't."

"Come on, guys. She's slow—I felt bad for her."

One of them moved around me—circling off my flank. It was a decent groove. I would've gone all the way around— kept the victim guessing—but I'll give him a couple points for trying.

A police cruiser drove by and stopped in front of the tobacco shop. I stepped in that direction.

The boys blocked me.

"Do you think he's gonna save you?"

"I just want to go home, guys. Come on, I've got a wife and kids. I said I was sorry."

"Maybe he should pay a tax, Billy. Maybe that, and we'll let him get on his way."

Hmmm. We hadn't been properly introduced, but "Billy" it turns out, was smart enough not to write gangster on his forehead.

"I don't have any cash, guys."

"What's in the bag?" Billy snatched it from my hand.

The cop was oblivious. Here I was, getting robbed less than fifty feet away, and he was—well, I don't know what the fuck he was doing over there, but he sure as fuck wasn't paying attention.

Billy dropped my sandwich pack on the sidewalk and stomped it with his heel. An unexpected tear welled in my eye.

I thought about a boy and his mother—the love she had for him, bringing that pack home and fixing up that treat. He didn't just stomp on those little sandwiches; he stomped on my fantasy of being loved, on having a mother who cared for me as more than a piece of flesh that she could sell to leering old perverts hungry for a taste of boy meat.

"He's fucking crying, Billy. What a bitch."

The leader saw my tears and pitied me—too bad I wouldn't return the favor. No remorse could erase the callousness he showed when he stomped my lil' Bluebird sandwich pack.

73

"Get the fuck out of here, faggot—and next time," Billy, who was soon to be brutally murdered, kicked me in the ass, "think before you open your fucking mouth."

That was close. I don't know where that emotion came from, but like I said, I ain't got no use for it. I could have lost it—settled up on the spot—and ruined everything.

It was almost an hour before they split. I guess they'd been waiting for something because when a car pulled up, a sense of ease came with it. Billy approached the driver, there was a quick exchange, and it was done—leaving the boys much happier than before.

Good for them—a bottle of booze freely given, plus whatever else they just scored. Looked like a party.

The boys climbed into a beat-up primer grey four-door, and I followed. I was thinking about how I wanted to handle this.

I'd recently picked up a nice little .38—a snub-nosed police special, Smith & Wesson—but I also had my hammer.

Hammers are good for releasing anger. A hammer says, I hate this motherfucker. I hate everything he represents, and I need to consummate that hate by blasting his fucking, sucking-up-my-air stink into little itsy bits of broken sandwich crumbs.

Sometimes I wonder if I'm honoring something when I express myself in a way that society and moral laws might call unnatural— taking a life.

Taking a life isn't waste; it's new ownership.

Maybe that's why I feel bigger after I make a move.

Is it so fucking hard to be kind? To answer when spoken to? To be helpful and generous when you can?

You never know when someone is hurting—or when they're capable of hurting you.

I followed them into a neighborhood of beautiful homes—not expensive, but cherished. A sense of pride lived in the community. Their car pulled into the driveway of what I'd call the least cherished house on the block. It looked close to abandoned—a dandelion in a field of flowers.

There were two other cars in the driveway and a motorcycle leaning against the fence. None of the vehicles looked capable of moving.

The front door was open. There was a screen, but it looked broken— hard to tell from the street, but probably unlocked. Then the music came on—loud, angry wails skanking through the windows, the door, and the seams of that house, spraying its vitriolic din all over the cherished homes around it.

Clang, clang, clang—noise puked on the neighborhood. A fucking shame—selfish little shits without a care for anyone but themselves.

I parked on the main street behind their house. I could've gone over the back fence and out the same way, but it was a nice evening, and the neighborhood was beautiful. So, I strapped on that little .38 and took a walk around the block.

I decided to leave the hammer in the car. I was gonna beat the fuck out of Billy's face, but his moment of kindness earned him a slightly less horrible death—still brutal, of course, just not the hammer.

I nodded pleasantly to a few folks—even stopped and chatted up the weather with a nice old woman who'd lived there her whole life. As I walked, I imagined myself with Debbie. I know we can't have children— or at least I don't think she can—but we could be happy here—at least, for as long as she lives. I don't think her people are blessed with long lives.

As I imagined, the screen door was torn and unlocked, the front door wide open. Tattoo-face slumped on the couch to my left. Two slugs to the chest—pop, pop. Drugged-out fucker was too high to see it coming.

The third boy—the one who laughed outside the store window—was just as stoned. That pissed me off. I didn't want 'em to wake up dead. I wanted 'em dead before they passed out.

I shook him, slapped his face a couple times—got an eye flicker— then drilled him. Two more—pop, pop, bitch.

Now, let me be clear: none of these were headshots. That's Bollywood bullshit. Heads are easy to miss. Even at close range, your target can jump, wiggle, or twist in a way that throws off the shot. Don't get me wrong—I'll make sure they're done for. But right now, I just need them out of action, and a couple of clean body shots does the job.

I walked past the turntable. They had some good old Southern California hardcore spinning—shit music, but at volume ten, it was perfect for covering gunshots and pissing off the neighbors.

I'll put on something classy before I leave—turn it down to a reasonable level.

I found Billy in the upstairs bathroom, a syringe on the floor at his feet.

Already dead.

I know there's a message in this, but I'm not sure if it's for my benefit or my detriment. This fucking punk makes fun of one of God's simpletons, then threatens me for trying to protect her. Yeah, he showed kindness, a flicker of empathy later, but he still stole my booze and fucked up my sandwich pack. He's a sinner—and in my opinion, due for a beat down. But when I show up at his door, God intervenes and gives him an easy out.

I'm not sure what to make of that.

I would've thought God wanted the boy punished—especially for making fun of Debbie. She's a fucking retard, man. There's gotta be a place in hell for that. Oh well. God's will, and all that. I don't give a fuck. As long as he's not upset at me.

I kicked Billy off the toilet, relieved myself, and then put one between his eyes. I know what I just said about headshots, but he was lying there real still, and I've got a steady hand—so… I didn't miss.

DINNER PARTY

When I got home, the house was jumping. The lights were on, and laughter spilled from the dining room. I heard Rachel's voice—she sounded happy. *I'm glad she was. I want the best for my little girl.*

They were sitting at our dining room table—a family heirloom passed down from my great aunt. At Rachel's right sat a boy, presumably from her school, wearing the black-and-gold letterman jacket of a Parkside Panther. To her left—King Dick himself, Tony, who greeted me as I walked in.

"There he is, the man of the house."

What the hell was he doing here?

"We were hoping you might cook us up a little something to eat, Wes, but since you hadn't come home, we got take-out."

They were dining on Chicken Delight.

I kept it together.

"Paula, I'm not familiar with your friend—how about an introduction?"

"Not familiar? Who you kidding, buddy. I was just telling Rachel and young Tyson here how I met you at the liquor store—" he mimed distress, "Help me! Help me! Ha!"

I forced a quarter-smile and turned to Rachel.

"And this young man—I'm definitely not familiar with him."

The kid ignored me and turned to the big dick. "Hey, Tony, you ever shot someone? I'm not sure if I could. You know—killing somebody and all."

"Well, Tyson, you look like a man who could handle himself in a pinch. We wouldn't let you see Rachel if we didn't think you could protect her. I believe you're a killer, son."

Am I going crazy? What the fuck is going on here? The guy fucking my wife is sitting in my house, having dinner with my daughter, telling this little shit he's a killer—and no one thinks this is odd?

Rachel put her hand on Tyson's thigh—*a little too close to his business.*

I needed to assert my authority.

"I'm sure anyone could pull the trigger if the stakes were high."

They turned and stared at me like I'd just shat myself in church.

Tony shook his head. "Do you honestly think you would've drawn down on those boys the other day? I saw the footage. You don't got it in you, Wes. You looked like you were crawling across the Sahara looking for water—or a fucking Slurpee."

The group laughed, Paula loudest of all.

"Speaking of which," Tony held his glass in the air, "I need a little refresher on my cocktail. How 'bout you get that going for me, huh?"

"Me too, yeah." Tyson raised his glass.

He was, at best, eighteen—barely cutting it, not a hair on that weak chin.

"Are you old enough to drink, Tyson?"

The boy looked to Tony.

"I'm carrying the badge, Wes. You worry about leather pumps and handbags; I'll worry about young Tyson, and his ability to imbibe."

As I walked out I saw Tony snuggle Paula—kiss her neck in a way that couldn't be mistaken for friendship. She looked back at me with the nasty satisfaction of someone who was gonna pay her husband back for a wrong he didn't commit.

Rachel didn't seem the least bit alarmed by their affection. I hadn't realized Paula had her that wrapped. I thought she had the intelligence to know better—and the heart to not see me hurt.

At 10:00, I was told I'd be driving Tyson home—Rachel would be riding along. I was tired, but it was better than letting the boy drive after drinking.

They'd been pounding booze since I got home—probably long before. Tony was the worst off. With each sip, his volume climbed, his words ran into each other. Sentences became long, sloppy slurs, and his hands moved across my wife as if they were looking for evidence.

"You take your time, Wessy... Make sure those kids get back safe— safe as kids can get back where they're going."

I didn't need this drunken buffoon to tell me how to take care of my family. If a man can't hold his liquor, he isn't a man.

"I think we'll be just fine, officer."

Tony grabbed me by the ears and lifted until only the tips of my shoes touched the floor.

"You're a fucking-little bitch, Wessy. You don't know shit about fine—I'll pull yer-fucking ears off."

Tyson and Rachel laughed as Paula stepped close, her face inches from mine, spraying vodka cranberry as she spoke. "You asked for it, Wormsie. Shoot that little mouth off, and that's what you get—eary, eary, ears. Ha!"

Tony let go with a final tug for emphasis. Paula stood by his side.

"All night long, you've been a real stick-in-my-mud, and now look at you. Tony's our guest—show him his respect."

"You did shoot your mouth off, Dad."

My ears felt like they'd been ripped off and sewn back on.

Tyson put his arm around Rachel. "He should've beat your ass, Mr. Wallace."

"Come on, Tyson-buddie." Tony, forced to sit back down, was losing to his own staggering. "He didn't know better—and you should respect her daddy."

"You're right, Tone." Tyson covered his ear in mock fear. "I wouldn't want you ripping my ears off. Ha!" He grabbed Rachel's hand. "Come on, Baby. Let's wait in the car before your dad gets his ass kicked."

They were sitting in the back, treating me like I a driver for hire.

"Where do you live, Tyson?"

He caught my eyes in the rearview, grabbed my daughter's face, and kissed her cheek. *I wasn't worth talking to.*

"Hey, guys. Can you knock that off and tell me where to go?"

"He lives across from the school, Dad. The green apartments on Palm."

"Oh, that's a nice little place. How long have you, uh—"

I glanced in the rearview. They were kissing, and his hand was sliding up Rachel's top.

"Hey, can you stop that?"

Tyson broke the kiss, looked at me, and then lifted her shirt, exposing her breasts.

"And what are you gonna do if I don't?"

"Tyson!"

"Stay out of it, Babe. I asked your old man a question."

He cupped her breast, his eyes locking on mine. He bent down and licked her nipple.

"Look, Tyson, I'm cool—but—"

"Cool? Fuckin, Tone was right, man. Your dad's a fucking bitch, Babe." He undid his pants. "Hey, Mr. Wallace, you ever see your daughter suck a cock?"

I didn't answer. I didn't look back. I didn't need to. The sounds were enough—his heavy breathing, my daughter choking as he held her down. I didn't have the balls to stop him. I was afraid.

Thank God for my pills—could you imagine having to face yourself unsedated, your cowardice crawling before your eyes? I was thankful he didn't screw her.

When we pulled up, Tyson got out without a word.

I was hoping Rachel would stay the night at his place, but she didn't. She stayed in the backseat, silent. I glanced once in the rearview mirror—that was enough. The lights on the highway were shameless in their exposure of her—hair a mess, lipstick smeared, and the unmistakable look of a woman who'd just been used.

When we got home, Rachel went straight to her room. That was the last I saw her that night. Later, as I passed her door, I heard music and the sound of her crying.

I doubt getting her mouth fucked in the back of my car was Paula's goal for her. It sure as hell didn't sound like she had much power when Tyson was choking her out. I thought Rachel was better than that.

Tony's car was still in the driveway. He was staying over.

Down the hall from our bedroom, there was a maid's supply room— just big enough to crash on the floor. I don't know why I didn't use one of the extra bedrooms. I was hating on Paula. But I guess I still wanted to be close—*habit.*

I grabbed a blanket from the linen closet and a pillow off the couch.

At just after midnight, Paula opened the door. She was naked.

"Tony wants you to come in."

"Not tonight, Paula. I'm tired."

She walked out but returned within moments.

"He's not asking."

I got up and followed her into our bedroom.

Tony was sprawled across the bed, eyes closed, his cock hanging large and flaccid between his legs. When I moved closer, he opened his eyes.

He sat up and nodded toward the small vanity mirror on my nightstand. On it, a rolled-up bill lay beside a line of what I assumed was cocaine. Paula handed him the bill, and he ran it down the white powder as he inhaled.

I didn't know people still did that stuff.

"Take your clothes off."

"Me?"

"She's already naked, you stupid fuck. Take your fucking clothes off, or I'll rip 'em off."

I took off my shirt and my pants but left my underwear on.

"All of it." He pointed at Paula. "I want to watch you fuck her."

"Tony, no."

"Fucking do it, bitch. There's no way you fucked him. Why are you still living here if she isn't his kid—why are you lying?"

"Baby, I told you. We've never had sex. Look at him—look at that little dick."

"That's fucking bullshit."

She handed me my clothes. "Wesley, get out of here—"

"No!"

He hit her with a pillow, a well-aimed shot that split her bottom lip. "I wanna see you fuck him."

Alcohol is a strange thing. They say it's a solvent—it'll make jobs, families, and good lives disappear. Maybe that's what happened to Tony's wife and kids—they were erased. Solvent, yeah, but also an adhesive. You get an idea in your head—crazy as it might be—like nobody could ever love somebody who wasn't physically attractive— and alcohol cements it. You can't shake it. You gotta ride it—until it lets go, until it's through with you. Tony couldn't see Paula staying with me. He didn't believe we'd never actually had sex, and no reason in the world was gonna chip that thought out of his head.

He stood, wobbling like a monster with an 8-ball for legs, and shoved me onto the bed. He yanked off my underwear, their removal met with great gales of laughter.

"Ha! Let me see it. Spread your fucking legs."

I did as he asked.

When he grabbed my balls, holding and bouncing them in his hand like ripe fruit at market, I tried to disconnect.

It didn't work.

"Does it get hard, little man?"

He pinched my cock, his index finger larger than my manhood. He grabbed at Paula.

"Suck that thing. I wanna see you ride it. Show me what you did."

When Paula put her mouth on me, it was as far from a sexual act as it could get. I've been more aroused at the dentist.

She bit, sucked, and licked in a futile attempt to arouse me, but it was no use. As he fucked her from behind, I felt her head push into my stomach, again and again, his drunken laughter filling the room.

At some point, she gave up on my cock entirely, resting her body against mine—a backstop for his lust.

I used to like her perfume—the scent of her skin, her warmth. I used to like being next to her, but not anymore. Marcy's taken her place.

He came and pulled out. Paula rolled off me, and I stood up. He flipped her onto her stomach and spread her legs. I could only assume this wasn't the first time tonight. Her anus looked used, her cunt swollen, practically distended.

I stood next to him, barely reaching his chin. His cock was no longer hard but not yet soft. He stroked it as he stared at my wife's ass.

"Take your pick, man."

I didn't understand.

"You can lick it off her, or you can clean it off me."

I knelt down and put his cock in my mouth.

As I told you before, I'm straight—and you can say, "Just keep telling yourself that, Wesley." But I mean it. I found my wife's used body more disgusting than his dick.

THE 'C' STANDS FOR CRAZY

I'm not sure how I slept in. The room was cold, the floor hard, and the pillow beneath my head was made for decoration, not comfort. Even so, it was late when I woke. If Marcy didn't go to work today, the shop would still be closed—two hours past its opening time.

I visited our bedroom. The bed was unmade, pillows and clothes scattered across the floor. An empty bottle of Evan Williams sat on the dresser, and the vanity mirror was still on the nightstand—minus the cocaine.

Wesley Wallace—maid to the morally depraved.

I began with the bed—pilling the pillows, brushing off the sheets, checking for wet spots, uncovering a lone black sock, and then shaking out the spread—*"What the fuck?"*

Tony's backup piece and holster hit the floor.

"How the hell do you forget your gun?"

I didn't touch it. I cleaned the room, rinsed the mirror, and walked out.

My meds make me dreamy sometimes, especially in the morning before I've eaten. Things aren't always what they seem. Maybe it wasn't even there—you know, wishful thinking and all that. But with each step, my mind kept returning to this image—me, larger than life, a superhero with unlimited power at my fingertips. All I had to do was touch the trigger, and it was mine.

I got dressed and went downstairs.

Two of Paula's dresses were lying on the table with a note: "*I need these taken to the cleaner—and drop off Tony's pants too.*" I didn't see the pants in the pile. "*We're going away for the weekend. I need them back by Friday.*"

Away for the weekend?

Rachel's door was still closed—the music low, just like last night.

Pretty sure it's a school day—she should be out of here or at least on her way by now. Oh, well. You know the drill. Keep my mouth shut. Don't rock the boat.

I found Tony's pants draped over a chair in the living room.

Faintly I heard the sound of typing, the familiar; Click, click, click— punch. How the hell do you forget your gun?

I wanted to impress Debbie. My plan was to wait outside her work and walk her to the bus. I'm not a stalker. Well, I have stalked—but only to do harm, not to creep out on some unsuspecting woman.

I've been to the grocery store every day. Debbie works Monday, Wednesday, Thursday, and Saturday until 8:00. She takes the number two bus up Grove, then walks to an apartment building on the outskirts of Little China. Her number's unlisted, and she lives alone. I was so proud of her when I found out.

This was new for me—she was part of a breed of human I didn't understand. I don't know what her people were capable of, but I was eager to learn.

Today was the day. I'd sit knee-close, maybe touch her hand, and walk her up the stairs to her door. I wanted to look my best.

I'd left a shirt at the cleaners—a good one. Bought it two years ago, wore it only twice: once, when I dispatched a young family broken down on the interstate—got a sprinkle of the kid's blood on the collar—and once, at a church social—a little mustard and a coffee spill. Both times,

I took it straight to the cleaners. It's a nice shirt, and I wanna keep it that way.

The dry cleaner was on the way to the shop. It was a family-run business that'd been there for years. I parked out front and walked in. A man stood ahead of me—fairly tall, blond hair, athletic build. I couldn't see his face, but something about him felt familiar—his body, his mannerisms. It wasn't like I knew him—nothing that simple. It felt like blood—like he was part of me. My brother.

I know how that sounds, especially coming from me—a man who admittedly rearranges the truth. But I'm not lying. It was the strangest feeling.

The cleaner handed him a dress shirt wrapped in polyethylene plastic on a wire-and-cardboard hanger—the type of shirt I would've bought. The cut was fashionable and the fabric, high quality.

How do I explain how I knew it was a man, even with my back turned and him stepping lightly into the cleaners? I can't. And I'm not going to tell you it was some innate predator's sense, because it wasn't. As crazy as it sounds, it felt like he was me, walking up behind me—I could see myself. His presence wasn't alarming. If anything, I felt comforted, like he understood me better than anyone ever had. It was as if he had seen all my faults, and loved me anyway.

I finished my transaction and turned around. I knew him—quite well. I smiled and offered him my hand.

"Good morning, Wesley. It's a pleasure to meet you."

The C stands for *Cornelius.*

Charles shook my hand and waited patiently while I dropped off my cleaning. Together, we walked outside and crossed the street into the park. We sat on a bench beneath a sprawling oak. For a while, we didn't speak. We didn't need to. There was no awkwardness, no urgency—just the quiet hum of he and I. Our lives intertwined.

When we finally spoke, it was in unison.

"I think I'm in love."

The woman on the next bench thought we were talking to her. She grabbed her things and scooted off.

"You're not our type!"

I'm not sure which of us thought it, but we both said it.

We tried to speak our separate minds but it was impossible to verbalize our thoughts. Every time we spoke, it was in unison. The harder we tried, the more we failed. Soon we were speed-talking nonsense, faster and faster, trying desperately to trip the other up, but it was no use. It escalated until we stumbled on the same word in the same breath—and gave up, falling into silence again.

Silence was best for us. Our inner voices could manage polite discourse.

Are you okay? I asked.

"Yeah, I'm doing alright—busy."

It's good to have something to do—idle hands and all that stuff.

"Yeah, I hear you man. I get in trouble when I don't get that mind going. I like that thing you're getting into—jailbait, it ain't my groove. but I can dig it."

I could say the same for you, buddy, it's not my groove, but I can dig it.

After a while, I knew it was time to leave, and so did he. We walked back to the car, and we kissed—a kiss of fraternal love. In that embrace, I felt his strength seep into me, mingling with my weakness. I felt as if I could do things that I couldn't before—take actions foreign to me, actions some might call barbarous or cruel. I felt as if I was more of a man.

I didn't want him to go.

"Wesley." His voice echoed in my head. *"I don't know if it's good*

for us to see each other—"

"I understand."

"But thank you for leaving the lights on."

He paused for a moment. There was something more, a line that he was hesitant to cross, and then he stepped over.

"And if I am you, there's a gun store on the corner of 14th and Pine. You can purchase ammunition there. The weapon you've been coveting is a .38 snub-nose police special—it'll get the job done. Never touch it with your bare hands, and if you clean it properly, no one will ever know you used it. You're a killer, Wesley. You have what it takes."

I smiled and thanked him—his words as naturally spoken as if they were my own. I checked my watch. Pine wasn't far. I knew the place—I drove by often.

There's a flower shop across the street. If they're open, I'll pick up a lily—a Stargazer for the object of my desire rose.

I was hoping Marcy went to work today.

ROCKED UP AND DEAD

She glanced at her watch—two and a half hours late.

The store looked as if it had been busy. Marcy fawned over a customer, treating her like royalty. The woman's purchase was impressive—six pairs of shoes and an ugly brown leather belt that'd sat there for years. As she left, she thanked me and offered Marcy prayers for her younger brother.

"What's the matter with your brother?"

She walked past me into the office. "I don't have one."

She perched on my desk, legs crossed—sheer nylons, short skirt.

"I need you to kneel at my feet."

I did.

"Remove my shoes. Caress each toe—soft kisses are allowed, but no moisture—keep those kisses dry. Do it now."

It felt good to be wanted again.

I took my time, grateful for each slight taste of her flesh.

Satisfied, she bade me stand.

"I like you, Wesley. I think we're going to get along just fine. You're a deviant after my own heart. How can you serve me better?"

"I was thinking about stopping my meds."

"Your meds? Enlighten me, Boss Man. How could that help me?"

"They've got me on this crap that blocks my emotions. It's supposed to help, but all it really does is flatten me out. I can't be me when I'm taking it—whatever *me* is. I gotta be better by now. They only gave it to me because I was struggling with my father's death—complicated grief or something. I don't know exactly what they meant. Waddell said *collusion*, but he's a tool, and most of his diagnoses come out of my mother's mouth. I bet if I stopped, I could feel again—*really* feel."

"What are you taking?"

I shared the list.

"*Zyprexa* is an antipsychotic."

"How do you know that?"

"I don't have a brother."

In her own way, she was being honest about her emotional defects. I get it—no need for details. Her knowledge was lived, not learned— guilt by experience.

Or as Charles might say, "this bitch is out of her fucking mind."

"Wesley, I think I have something that might help you—and better serve me."

She opened a large cloth purse and handed me an imitation cock— a penis extender—flesh-like, firm yet flexible, with a ball strap for added security. It was impressive—a confidant man's royal blue.

"You ever owned one of these?"

"I've looked at them before."

"But you never bought one? Surely your wife brought it up at some point?"

"No. She's never been attracted to me, and I've never strayed outside my marriage. You can't just date a woman and whip something like that out on the first go-around."

"It sounds like you've put some thought into it."

"Not really. I can get myself off—but I'd wear something like that if the woman I was with demanded it."

"Don't even think about it, creep. I don't want that plastic dick shoved in me—probably causes cancer. Besides, I was thinking along other lines. Put it on."

She returned to her place on the desk—overseeing her older protégé.

"That strap goes around your balls—holds it tight. That's right. You're lucky they're big. I think you're gonna like this."

She was right. It fit easily—not uncomfortable at all—and I liked the way it changed my outline. I felt powerful.

"Is it too big?" I asked.

"No. It's 6.5. Bigger than average, but not too big at all."

"I bet you've had bigger, huh?"

"Come on, dude. I'm trying to help you—don't be a fucking pervert. Walk it around. See how it feels."

She took out her phone, snapped a few pics, and shot a quick video of me—hands on hips, striking a pose.

"Jerk it off."

"Does it cum?"

"Are you fucking kidding me? It's plastic, moron."

"I didn't know. Could've had some sort of shooting thing in it."

"Just stroke it."

It felt good. I pulled it from the bottom up—ran my thumb across the head.

I wonder if Charles' cock gets hard when he's—

"Yep!"

Shit. His voice was in my head.

"You know it does, Wessy. Came in my pants once. Beating the shit out of this old man—cock shot off like a rocket!"

Oh my, God. Did she hear him?

Marcy was unfazed. If she heard it, she didn't acknowledge it.

"It's just you and me, brother."

They can't hear you?

"Ha! If they do, you'll find yourself back in Greenwood. Hey, that's a nice dick—navy blue, huh? Just like mine."

"Put your pants on, Wesley. See how it rides."

"Fuck that. Take hers off, see how she rides."

I raised my hand to grab Marcy's hair, throw her to the floor, and take what's mine. But then I realized that thoughts didn't have to be actions—especially when they were coming from him.

I stifled Charles.

"Go, on. Close it up."

I couldn't zip my pants. The penis was poorly behaved. I pushed it down, but it popped back up. Flaccid wasn't in its design.

"Tuck it down the side, Boss Man."

"Which side?"

"I don't know—try one side at a time."

"I like it on the right, but damn, look at that. There's a big bulge in my pants."

I checked the mirror. Thankfully, I was wearing jeans—my slacks wouldn't have held it down.

"Taming the monster."

Shit, Charles' voice bled through.

"What was that?"

"Nothing, I was just—"

"Hello?"

Someone was in the shop. I hadn't heard them come in.

My voice dropped. "One minute, please." There was a touch of Charles in it. I started to remove my penis, but Marcy blocked my hand.

"Go like that," she whispered. "Be the big man. Let her see it."

Hell, why not? What's the worst that could happen? "You know, Angie, I went into that shoe store the other day, and the manager had a big ol' cock." Jeez, I'd love to hear that go down.

I strutted into the showroom, confidence bouncing against my thigh.

"Good morning, Miss. How may I help you?"

My voice carried authority and power—*shit, is that what having a nice cock does for you? I guess I never got it before. All those jokes about overcompensating? Now I know why.*

She was cute.

"I saw your ad in the *Park Gazette*—thought I'd check out your selection. I'm looking for something for the evening."

I pushed my crotch out slightly—not too much, just enough. "My selection, huh? See anything you like?"

We shared a laugh.

Shit, Marcy didn't just buy me a dick. She bought a whole new me.

The woman left with two pairs of shoes and signed up for future specials.

"Make sure to call me if anything comes in, okay?"

I shook her hand, lingering for a moment and meeting her eyes. "I'll make sure to do that Miss... Halverson."

"Judy."

"I'll be sure to do that, Judy."

She paused at the door, cracked it open, then quickly closed it again. "Are you okay?"

"Yes, I think so. There's a man outside—he seems crazy. He asked me for money, and when I said no, he called me a rude name and..." She hesitated, peering through the glass. "There he goes. There..."

She stepped out, and I followed her—walking her to her car. The man she mentioned shuffled up the alley behind my store, likely heading for the trash cans. She thanked me again and promised to return.

Marcy was waiting at the counter. "How'd that go, big dick."

"It was great—I think I could've done her." I glanced at myself in the mirror. "Do you think she'd know this was fake if she didn't—"

Bang!

A loud crash echoed from the alley, an empty metal trash can slammed against the back door.

"It's that fucking bum. He was harassing Judy. Come on."

"What?"

"Come on!"

Charles' voice whispered in the background, low and insistent.

"I hate these motherfucker's. We should do 'em all, dude—every motherfucking one of 'em. You'd be doing God a service by taking 'em out—it's destiny, Wessy. No more rancid food and cardboard bedclothes. Come on, Baby. Let Daddy show you how to kill."

I cut through the break room and opened the door to the alley.

"Hey! Get the fuck out of those cans."

He looked up at me like a cornered animal—dirty, bent, slobbering. His body was weak, his muscles hollow—a dumpster diving skeleton with crooked teeth and yellow eyes.

"It's not your fucking world, dude—it's trash—'member? You tossed it."

"Fuck him."

I didn't hesitate. Didn't weigh his worth. No worth—bones and trash.

"You don't think about taking a shit, dude; you just drop it. Shit this motherfucker. Shit him right out."

There was a broken broom handle by the door—snapped jagged when I pulled down the bathroom grate. I held it, like a baseball bat in my hands, and I stepped to the plate.

"Do it, Wessy! Swing!"

I broke his arm.

The second blow cracked his skull. The third, his other arm.

I smashed him across the face—a swing worthy of a real big-leaguer—and struck again. I never knew air could taste so sharp, so fresh, as it did when he fell beneath me. I inhaled his pain.

Fuck him.

"Hold up, Wessy. Slow your roll." Charles purred. "This, my friend, is called an exchange of power. And you? You're running the bank. Take it in, killer. Collect it. This motherfucker's bill just came due—cha-ching, cha-ching, motherfucker, cha-ching."

My breath roared like an engine, inflating my heart. My arms, great pistons of violence—pumping, spewing destruction with every blow.

"Breathe. Take it. Take his life. Take it. Fuck this piece of shit."

I stabbed him in the stomach with the jagged end of the broom handle. Pulled back, then stabbed again. Over and over until his skin ceased to resist. I stood over him, panting—blood dripping from the wood.

I leaned down, and let Charles say his goodbyes.

"Still your trash, motherfucker? Whose world is it now, you wretched piece of shit."

Marcy came up behind me, her hand light on my shoulder.

"I think I just made me a monster."

Her laugh snapped me into reality—drove Charles away.

There was a man, lying at my feet, gasping for air. Dying.

"Go get your car, Wesley. We'll put him in the trunk."

"He's not dead."

"Would you prefer he was?"

"No, but I—shouldn't we call somebody?"

"Get your fucking car. Let's get him out of here before somebody comes."

I hustled down the alley.

"Call somebody? Ha, that's rich. 'Excuse me, Mr. officer, I just beat and stabbed a man for digging in my trash. Could you uh, send someone over to pick him up?' Come on, Wessy, use those balls. We got work to do."

He was dead by the time I returned.

I don't know if you've ever picked up a body once the life's gone out of it, but it ain't easy. I was glad Marcy was there to help. Even then, we had to fold him over the trunk like a bag of wet laundry and flip his legs in.

I stood there, looking down at him. I felt good—accomplished.

When was the last time I felt like this? Second grade, Miss Ann's class, the spelling bee. I'm a champion—a fucking gladiator.

Marcy put her hand up under his shirt, dipped her fingers in his blood, and smeared it across my face—catching the corner of my mouth.

"Fuck Marcy! He could have AIDS. What are you doing?"

"Quit being a bitch." She lifted her skirt and slid her nylons down. Her bloody fingers disappeared between her legs. "I'm fucking dripping, Wesley."

She pulled her hand out and wiggled her fingers. "Want a taste?"

The blood and her juices were still warm.

PANIC IN THE PLAYHOUSE

We dumped the body near the monastery along the coast road. It tumbled down a ravine into a grove of brambles, out of sight.

"Do you think it's good to have our phones on?"

Emotionless, she stared at me, unconsciously biting the tip of her thumb. A sweet young girl with dashboard lights in her eyes.

"What if they ping us or something? There was a tower back there."

"You spend a lot of time alone, Wesley?"

"Like 'me' time?"

"Jesus Christ, Wessy. I can't with this gay-ass shit. That little cunt's fucking with you—yanking your chain. You took out the trash, motherfucker. Nobody's pinging us—put your eyes on the road— goddamn it!"

My right wheels kissed the dirt as I tore through the corner. Marcy's nails clicked on the dash. I deepened my tone, roughing up the edges— gave it that Charles thing.

"Ha! Fucking cold-case, babe—getting all pinged up and questioned, you know."

"Now you're just scaring me—how many of you are in there?"

"It's just me."

"And who's that, Boss Man?"

"It's Wesley."

"And when your voice changed? When you wasted that bum?"

"It was me, Marcy. Come on, you were standing right there—you saw it."

"Me, Wesley?" she paused. "Right?"

"Give me the fucking phone. What is this, high school?"

He pulled the car over, put it in park, and shut off the motor.

"Look, sugar tits. Stop with the twenty fucking questions—you ain't Freud. It doesn't matter how many fucking people we got up in here—unless you're looking for a gang bang. Then we gotta whole crew."

He twisted in his seat, his left hand sliding down between her legs—no resistance. His right hand fisted her hair, pulling just enough for hard tension's sake. He leaned close, his breath carrying the taste of blood and the rotting odor of tobacco compost. With the tip of his tongue, he licked the corner of her mouth, his voice a low, menacing growl.

"You're not the one I wanna fuck, sweetheart, but if I gotta, I'll drill a hole in you an army of monkeys couldn't fill. You need to mind your own fucking business. You wanna stick around? Great. You wanna run? Have at it. Either way, you're an accessory to murder. So just sit there, clicking your fucking press-on nails, and shut your fucking mouth."

She pushed her crotch against his hand, her breathing deepening—slow and steady.

"Oh, look at that. You like it when Daddy rubs that little, pussy, huh?"

"Yes, Daddy."

"Well, that's good to know, Baby. But I like to watch. You wanna give

me something to look at, go ahead. I'll be more than grateful."

He undid his jeans and pulled off the rubber cock. "Here—" he tossed it onto her lap. "Save this for another go."

She reached for it without hesitation. He bit her shoulder—uneven teeth drawing vicious pin-pricks of blood.

"I like my ass fingered when I'm getting my cock sucked. You got that?"

"Yes, I hear you..."

My cellphone rang. *I told her the tower was too close.* It was a desert area code—I hoped it wasn't something with my mother. Charles retreated and I stepped in.

"This is Wesley."

"Little Wes?"

"*Bradberry*— " Charles whispered his contempt. *"Give me the phone. Let me talk to that Dallas Rains piece of shit. I'll drown him in tanning butter, that motherfucker*— "

"No. Not now."

"Wes? Is that you?"

Charles sneered in my head. *"Kill him."*

Come on man, don't do this to me.

"*Do what, Wessy? Let somebody roll over us... again?*"

I slapped myself—a hard, stinging blow—*pull it together, buddy—come on, pull it together.*

"Wes? Hello? Can you hear me?"

"Put it on speaker, Babe."

Marcy's voice grounded me. Her hand on my leg. I clicked over.

"I'm sorry, Mr. Bradberry. It's a busy day here."

"I bet, up to your eyeballs in high-heels and garter belts."

"We don't sell garter belts."

"And that's why I haven't been in. Look, Wes, I'm bringing a few people by to see the house. Maybe Tuesday or Thursday. That pool shack out back? We're taking it down next week."

"My office?"

"Office—yeah, that's cute. That playhouse isn't worth fixing—the roof's shot."

"*Playhouse? My sanctuary? Fuck this faggot.*"

Charles sang in my head. *"Somebody's getting their ass kicked. Somebody's getting their ass kicked*— "

"Stop it."

"Can't do it, Wes. The ball's already rolling. Hey, do you know why Paula's not answering her phone?"

"No, I uh…"

"Oh, well. I'll catch her later. *Ciao*, sport."

He hung up.

"Who the hell was that asshole?" Marcy caressed my thigh.

A wave of sickness rolled through me—a tight pain in my chest, my neck locking up. I couldn't breathe.

"I want to go home."

"Home?" She squeezed my leg. "Hang on a minute, Baby. It's okay, just breathe for a second."

Panic attack. Fuck. Fuck. Fuck. Fuck. Put my head where my feet are at. Shoes—socks. Pants against my legs, shirt, wheel, hands on the leather—feel my fingers, feel my feet. I can't breathe. I can't breathe. Smack my lips—one, two, three, four. Breathe. Four in. Hold seven. Out eight. Again. Again. Again. Come on, come on, I got it. I got it.

Okay, okay… okay.

My heartbeat skipped—every six beats a warning—thump, thump, thump—bump, bump, bump… blurp. *Ughhh. I fucking hate this.*

Put my head where my feet are at at—put my head where my feet are at. I can't breathe. I can't breathe. Okay. I got it. I got it. I got it.

Here I am. Okay.

Deep… Deep… In and out. Let it go… Let it go. Let it go….

She pulled down the visor and put on some lipstick, blind to the terror I'd just endured.

"Can I smell that?" I asked, my breath slowly evening out.

"This?" She held up the gold tube, her eyes narrowing slightly. She waved it under my nose, the scent of rose instantly calming me.

It's gonna be okay—I'm okay.

"That smells nice, Marce—innocent, like rain in the morning."

"You're a strange little man, Wesley."

"Yes." My heart returned to normal. "Yes, I am."

Waddle once asked me if I ever lost track of time. Yeah, but it's not like that. It's not like I'm instantly transported from one place to another. I just don't remember how I got away from where I was—especially when a situation was uncomfortable or I was under stress. He called it disassociation. I called it a case of the splits.

"You okay, Boss Man?"

"Yeah, I guess I was just a bit rattled."

"It's not every day you get to kill someone."

"Huh?" I'd forgotten about the bum. Charles' voice in my head had gotten so loud—the volume pumped. "Jesus, yeah. I was so wrapped up in myself, I forgot all about that guy."

"That dude on the phone must be some prick to have that kinda power."

Power. That's what Charles said, right? Take it. I wonder... would offing Bradberry give me that same boost?

"Mmm—hunh."

I told Marcy about my home situation—*not all the details; nobody needs that*—but enough about Bradberry and losing my place.

"Do you think your mother would be selling if he wasn't pushing?"

"No. My mom likes to threaten—it's her way of keeping control. But she never follows through unless you drive her. I remember when I realized that. If I acted scared and worried, she'd just dangle it in front of me, wave me around on a string, then move on. But if I ever pushed back, questioned her threats, she'd hammer me—no matter what the cost."

"What if Bradberry was out?"

"What do you mean?"

"Don't play dumb with me, Wesley. You know exactly what I mean."

"That's what I'm talking about, motherfucker. Listen to this little slut, Wessy—let's cook that prick. Fuck him."

I was getting used to his voice in my head.

"I don't know, Marcy. This isn't some street bug—Bradberry's a player. He's known. They'd come looking."

"Tell me about him."

CHARLIE'S ANGEL

I know where she sits—behind the driver, one hand on the passenger pole, a sweet hello or a smile for everyone who boards. I can't do that, man. I don't have it in me. I look at people like targets—victims waiting to be victimized. She doesn't. Debbie is uncomplicated and pure, unburdened by an abundance of moving parts. And while she might look like a simpleton to you, that's only because you've never seen an angel—a thing so pure that evil can't exist within it. They don't look like us.

They don't hate like I do.

The driver stopped short. A truck veered into our lane. What if our man wasn't looking—if he'd glanced away for just a second? Little things like that change everything. It's why some kids get loved, and others get fucked in the ass by wicked old pederasts with yellow skin and shit-stained pants. And what about this—what if our driver saw it coming but carried on, streamlining us into a world of hurt?

My mother saw. She saw, she sold, and she dressed me for bed—put a fucking bow on it.

What's the thinking in a deal like that?

Oh well. I dust myself off, get this thing going. Let that old shit go. Live some kind of regular existence. Me and my girl.

Fuck it—past ain't got me.

I leaned back in my seat—straightened my collar.

I was thinking back to that first day—Debbie's name tag hanging askew, eyes to match—working in that grocery store. Those boys laughing, teasing—her smile never faltered. She was so careful with their things, treating those assholes with the utmost respect. Me? I'd have thrown their shit to the ground, stomped their fucking eggs, shattered the glass and rubbed their fucking faces in the shards—and I did, in my own way. But not her. She's better than me.

I never tried to be good. I knew early on there wasn't any fixing me—I am what I am. But when I stood in that line, my hate dissolved in her eyes, and for a moment, I felt peace. I'm not saying she'll heal me. No—I don't deserve that. But I believe she could keep my hand off the trigger—keep the gun out of my mouth. Not healed, but delayed—her purity holding my filth at bay.

I boarded the bus on Electric—sat a seat away from her usual spot, and counted the streetlights to the grocery. Debbie's stop: five lights. I had to get a little heavy with the old broad sitting next to me. Nothing noticeable—I didn't want to seem like a threat—but I crowded her a bit until she moved. Once she was gone, I took up two spaces—three, actually. I wanted to be able to slide over—play the gallant, when Debbie arrived.

She's so fucking cute.

The door opened, and there she was, wearing her Charlie's Angels T-shirt—retro edition from the local Jumbo Mart. It was rocking. Big smile for the driver. A wave to the lady I'd chased away.

I slid over to give her room. I could smell her sweat—not overpowering, just enough to know she'd been working. I don't know if you've ever been satiated by the scent of someone you love, but there was something between us—something cellular. Breathing her was like breathing life unaltered. I could exist off that.

I thought about being the one to bathe her, washing her hair, tucking that sweet little puddie into bed. I know it ain't right to think about her like that, but I can't help how God made me—or the attraction He Himself instilled.

I kept to myself for the first block or two. Yeah, I tossed out a couple of smiles and a glance, but on the whole, I let her settle into her routine, before I approached. We hit a bump in the road, and as we got sorted, I made eye contact.

"I like your shirt," I said. "Real cool."

She looked down at her chest, like she'd forgotten what she had on. Then she looked up at me and smiled. I'll be fucked if I didn't blush.

I slid an inch or two closer—not touching, but close.

"Do you like Charlie's Angels?" I said.

"I watch it with my grandmother. Do you like it?"

"I do. You remind me of them—an angel, riding on the bus."

She touched her hair and sat taller in her seat. She was interested. I pushed, but not too hard.

"I bet you can't guess my name."

She looked me over for a moment. It was hard to meet her gaze. I felt dirty—like she knew what I wanted.

"Is it Robert?"

"No. Why did you pick that?"

"My dad's name is Robert."

I lightly brushed her leg with the back of my hand—incognito. Fucking electric, man.

"Do I look like your daddy?"

"Whoa! Rein it in, cowboy."

I pulled back my hand and looked around the bus. Wesley's voice was swirling around me. I covered my eyes with my palms, tried to blink him off, then pushed my hair back. He was still there.

"Now you know how I feel when you're screaming in my ear. At least I'm not telling you to bash her fucking head in."

"Fuck you, man. Don't say that."

"Inside voice, guy. She can hear you."

Debbie might have been able to hear, but she was oblivious—"My dad is big. He has dark hair. He comes on Sundays."

"Does he?"

"Uh, huh." She brushed a gnat away. "He rides a motorcycle."

I leaned closer hoping the proximity would keep Wesley away. It didn't.

"What's she wearing, Charles? Eau de la Tard?"

"You need to watch your mouth, motherfucker."

"You know you just said that out loud."

"Then stop fucking talking to me."

"Seriously, dude. You're blowing it."

Debbie turned away—not mad. There were things to see through the window. People to smile at. I sat on my hands, bit my lip.

Please—don't fuck this up for me, Wesley. I need this.

"All right. I was just screwing around. It's strange being in your head. I thought I was messed up."

As Wesley bowed out, I dropped my keys on the floor and picked them up. It caught her attention.

"Jesus, was I just talking to myself?"

"I think so."

"Do you ever do that?"

There it was, that sweet smile—simple, effortless, benign. "Sometimes I think out loud."

"Ha! Me too. I'm a writer. Sometimes I think of the story in my head, and I say it out loud. You must have thought I was very rude. I apologize."

"That's, okay."

She was back. The trouble of a moment before was left on the corner of 188th and Dawson.

I was pretty sure I had her.

I looked out the window like I was searching for something, then I moved to the opposite side—which, if I don't say so myself, was a touch of romantic genius.

I caught her smiling at me, playing with her hair, and I played coy—strong with a touch of vulnerability—giving her the illusion of the upper hand.

I pushed the next-stop button before she did. Just in case. I didn't want anyone thinking I was following her.

I'd recently learned a new definition—neurotypical. That's what they call men like me. Debbie is a woman who has Down syndrome—it does not have her. You don't usually see mixed couples, but it does happen, and in my opinion, it's none of their fucking business who I want in my life. She's on her own, working and getting around by herself. I ain't trying to get with some bitch with complex needs—although there's nothing wrong with that either. But people do judge.

I walked to the back doors and grabbed the bars. Debbie always exited from the front. In my pocket, I had an address written on a scrap of paper—the building next to hers.

I got off the bus and stood like I was lost—look at the paper, scan the area, back to the paper—a man just trying to find his way. Debbie walked up to me and smiled.

"Do you know this place?" I held out my prop, the address written clear: 236 Hansen St. "I seem to be a bit turned around."

She took it, squinting at the writing. "That's my street."

"I have a friend that lives there. Is it far? Walk or cab?"

"It's not far. I walk through the park."

"Would you mind if I join you? We could keep each other company."

She hesitated—trying to figure me out, sum up the working parts, and see where I fit in her world. I half expected her to blow me off, but I guess she found something to her liking. She held out her hand.

When she spoke, it was slow and careful, like she wanted to get the words right. "My name is Debbie, Debbie Garson—I'm 27 years old."

Her palm was rough but not unpleasant—if anything, the crease in her flesh gave me more to feel.

"It's a pleasure to meet you, Miss Debbie. Charles C. Stinson. I'm 45—18 years your senior, and the C stands for cuddly."

"Ha!"

Her laugh lit the path ahead.

She was a wonderful companion—pointing out her favorite tree, a shaved poodle in a pink hat and sweater, the lake where the boys sail their boats. We found three things we both liked: birds, rain, and being out after dark.

When we passed the small rose garden near the gardener's shack, I reached over and lightly grazed her hand. She looked at me, smiled, and grabbed mine in return. Her grip was strong and capable, her hands not as rough as I thought. I wanted her to know that I was worthy—worthy of protecting her, of being in charge—so I squeezed harder.

"You're squishing my fingers."

I loosened my grip—just a touch. "Boyfriends have to be strong."

"Boyfriend?"

"Maybe, one day. If you like me."

We walked silently for a bit—past the pond and the vendors. I waited for her to speak.

"Do you like chocolate?" she said.

"I do. I like the peanut butter cups and caramels."

"My grandmother gave me peanut butter cups on my birthday. I like those too...and peppermints."

She stopped in front of the swing set—an old, rusted metal monstrosity with real chains and leather seats. I stepped through the sand and sat down on the swing—my ass barely squeezing between the chains.

"Push me," I said.

"Push you?"

"You look very strong to me. I bet you're the best pusher."

"I am."

She laughed as she placed her hands on my back. I stayed stiff, her hair willfully teasing my neck with every shove. I sailed above the hedges and the trees—so high I had to ask her to stop.

At her doorstep, I said my goodbyes—had every intention of leaving—and followed her upstairs.

Don't judge me for not being able to walk away. You don't know what it's like to be free of pain. People think booze erases the past, but it doesn't—it's a stew of despair, with hurt floating just below the surface of the drunk. You don't know what it's like to have thirty-seven years of burden not just lifted, but replaced—scars removed, fresh skin in their stead. You can't walk away from that. You can't.

Her apartment was bare—a few poorly tended plants, dried flowers, and a small kitchen table with two chairs. On the wall hung a bulletin board with "Debbie" spelled out in pink cloth letters and rhinestone diamonds. It was crowded with pictures of her friends and a scraggly orange tabby who'd passed from old age a year ago.

A portable record player sat on the table in the living room, its sides covered with stickers.

"Do you like music?" I asked.

"It's my favorite," she said, picking up an album and holding it to her heart.

"Like chocolate and birds, and being out at night?"

"Yes. I like all those things."

I knew the record she held—saccharine power-pop, recorded before she was born. I'd never had a turntable of my own, but at youth camp, Friday night mixers were a thing. I didn't do much mixing—I was uncomfortable around the girls—but I'd sit next to the turntable, fascinated by the DJ.

She placed the record on and dropped the needle into the groove. It skipped slightly, spun a touch slower than usual, then picked up speed— a Sunny Day Heart Break.

"A thousand stormy days say I love you. Wind and the rain and I know you're gonna stay. Out comes the sun and you leave me—our love must be a winter thing. Our love must be a winter thing."

"Do you like to dance?" She grabbed my hand and pulled me to my feet.

I didn't know what to do. I've never danced before.

Wesley stepped in.

"Don't worry, buddy, I got you." *I could feel his hands in mine.* "Can you feel it? It's a backbeat. You're clapping on the two and the four. *One, and TWO, and three, and FOUR."*

I counted out loud.

"Quietly—in your head now, killer. Step. Clap. Step. Clap. Keep it real simple. You be the groove; let her flow over you. Nothing special. No big moves."

At first, I was clumsy—every step a miss, every clap late. But then the beat pulled me in—controlled me. Once I let go, the groove came easy.

I could watch her now—swaying and stepping. She was worse than I was, and her lack of rhythm made me adore her all the more.

"She's beautiful, Charles. I can see why you like her."

I told you, man. I told you she was perfect.

She twirled once, then again, and again—the third time, she fell into my arms. I held her there, still swaying, and then I kissed her—a soft peck on her lips. She tasted like pizza and forgiveness.

"I'm not a good dancer," I said.

"You're a good kisser." She was breathing heavy, slightly winded. "Kiss me again!"

As I kissed her, my hand slid across her body—smooth, strong moves, searching my way.

"I like the way you feel, Debbie."

She closed her eyes and leaned into me. I'd never wanted anything as much as I wanted her.

"It's time to go, Buddy."

Wesley was right. I stepped away.

I checked my watch—the time unreadable. "It's getting late," I said. "I should go."

"Don't you like me?"

"Of course I do, but when boys and girls kiss a lot, they want more."

"You're as old as me, Charles."

"I'm older than you."

"I know that. Kiss me more. I like it."

I moved away—the distance awkward, noticeable, and unwanted. It hurt to leave her.

"How about this: let's call this a date, and I'll meet you again."

"You don't like me?"

"I like you so much that I can wait."

"No dessert before dinner."

"Right. Dinner first—a few dates, and then dessert."

"Sometimes, I eat dessert first." She licked her fingers.

Simpleton, my ass. She knew what she was doing. She kissed me again—pushed her body against me—so sweet, so pure.

Fuck it.

I pushed her down on the bed and unbuttoned her pants. She helped me, urgently kicking her legs free. I took off my shirt and trousers. Her innocence becoming a dark haze vibrating below me as my want grew. I took a handful of her hair and forgot who she was....

I take it you ain't never been raped—never been held down, sold by a loved one, or got so twisted up you mistook submission for compliance. Fucking? That's easy. But being touched, caressed, loved—it hurts. I'd never been intimate with another person in my life. I knew how to take, use, hurt, and be done with. I knew how to kill.

I didn't want to do it—not to my Debbie. But instinct overruled.

I am an animal.

"Open that fucking mouth, Baby."

She tried to push me away. She didn't mean it. She wanted this.

I fed her, forcing her to suck, to swallow.

"That's it, bitch. Take that fucking cock—take it."

I could feel my release building, muscling its way through my body.

"You're hurting me! Charles!"

She struggled to get away, but I held her in place. I wanted to cum.

"Stop it!" Wesley's voice tore through me like a volt up my spine. "Charles! Stop it!"

I froze—a dog pulled up on his master's leash. What the fuck—Oh God, what was I doing? Debbie. My sweet Debbie. I hurt her. I fucking hurt her.

I buried my head in my hands.

"Dude, you can't treat her like that!"

"Fuck, man. I didn't know… I'm sorry."

"You've got to be gentle—easy, Charles. You love her."

I've never done this before. It hurts. I wanna die.

"It's okay, just breathe, buddy. Most guys don't want to die until they're way into the relationship."

"It's not funny! I hurt her."

"You didn't hurt her—just shocked, scared is all. She's still here."

I thought she was gone.

She leaned over and kissed me—"you scared me, Charles."

"I'm sorry. I've never made love before."

"Love me?"

I was glad Wesley was there.

"Let her lead, brother. You don't have to be in charge. She knows what to do."

"Lay next to me, Charles?"

I did as she asked—turned toward her and held her. Her hair carried the scent of cheap strawberry shampoo.

"Will you be my boyfriend?"

"Yes, I'd like that."

"I like cuddling and kissing."

She stood, and I was both pained and fascinated by her innocence. My body bore the scars of a life I didn't ask for—shot, stabbed, burned, raped and abused since I was young. She was unblemished and whole.

She lay down on the bed and held the covers up, inviting me in. I climbed in beside her.

Her body pressed against mine.

I kissed her neck.

"Do you ever cry, Charles?"

"Yeah." I touched a tear to my finger and pressed it gently against her lips. "Sometimes I do."

JAILBAIT

I've always liked older men. At first, it was the comfort and the safety they provided. Then, it was the way they fucked. Young boys act as if they have something to prove—flexing and hammering as if it was a contest to see how raw they can leave you, like their marathon pounding somehow equates to satisfaction. I'm not saying I've never gotten off with a boy my age, but it's easier with a man of experience and confidence. Older men fuck like they know they're good. They don't care if you don't. They're not trying to prove anything. They use you to please themselves and assume that you've never had better. I like that. I like being used. I feel better about me when they cum.

In my early teens, I was a geek, a prude, a shy little girl who performed the part of untouchable junior high school innocence, but beyond that, I was in a relationship with my English teacher—Mr. Merriweather—a man four years older than my father.

My relationship with Old Merry started innocently enough. I was his classroom aide—grading papers, running to the copier, a bit of this and that. Then I started noticing how willing he was to do things for me.

One day, as I graded papers, he set a pack of Marlboro Reds on my desk.

"What's this?" I asked.

He smiled at me sheepishly like a little boy caught doing something bad, and in that moment, I felt the power shift. With that one relationship defining, and potentially career ending move, he'd put me in charge of his life.

He stammered. "The other day, I smelled smoke on your sweater and thought you might like those."

"Reds?" I lifted the pack and tapped it, holding his gaze. "You thought I smoked, Reds?"

"I didn't know. I... uh, guessed."

"Well, you guessed lucky this time."

I opened the package and popped a smoke into my mouth—the butt end sliding seductively across my lipstick and between my teeth.

He prayed that I wouldn't light it.

I'd never been in that position before. Men had always been in charge of me—never me over them. Until that moment, I'd felt powerless. But my awakening pushed me into a new state of being.

Yeah, I get it—you're sitting there reading this crap, doubting that a seventeen-year-old girl would have this sort of awareness. A bit mature for my age, huh? Don't forget—I plied my grandfather with booze to get him to screw me, and I was wiggling around in Father Hezekiah's lap when I was still in pigtails. It's called genius and depravity—a product of genetics and sexual abuse. A potent development cocktail when delivered in proper doses.

Wesley has no idea I understand him as well as I do. I'm the poster girl for disassociation—escaping to greener pastures while a fat, hulking pig of an uncle smothered me with his nude bulk. Greenwood. I was patient zero in their new youth program. I know my way around antipsychotics and old perverts who think young pussy is on the menu.

And I'll tell you this—if something goes wrong, if the hammer falls, I'll be the first to lower my eyes, stain my shirt with tears, and blame it all on that older white male, Mr. Wesley Wallace, who groomed me and forced me into his evil ways.

When I first realized I was in control of old Merryweather, I felt a touch of uneasiness, like I was in danger, left out in the open during a great storm. Then I shook it off and stepped into it. I took comfort in the role. I stretched out and tested how far I could push it.

"What else are you smelling, Mr. Merry?"

"Sometimes I smell your perfume before you come into the room." He wrung his hands as he spoke, nervously awaiting the abuse that he hoped would come. "I know, I can't really, but I'm familiar with your scent."

"My scent? I bet you'd like to buy me some—wouldn't you?"

"Yes. Yes I would."

"Cherry—that's what I wear. Write it down."

He took out his phone and typed it in, his hands shaking.

"You got that, *Cherry*?"

"Yes, yes. I got it."

"That's a good boy."

Men are so fucking easy. You know what they want—let them think they can have it, as long as they do what you say.

I moved to his chair—a brown leather business roller that he must have brought from home. I sat down and spun it until I was facing him.

I almost never wore skirts—always pants. But my mother, who always laid out my clothes, had set out a grey wool skirt that morning— cut six inches below my knees for modesty's sake. I spread my legs in front of him and I pulled up that skirt until, with bulging eyes, he caught a glimpse of my white cotton panties.

"I'm gonna ask you again, Sir. What else are you smelling?"

"I'm sure I don't know what you mean."

I slowly closed my legs, watching his eyes as I did. They were locked onto my flesh—I could lead him anywhere. I pointed to the floor between my legs, and without a word, he followed my command to kneel.

"Stay." I said.

I walked over to the door separating his classroom from the hall, turned off the lights, and checked the lock.

Mr. Merry had once told me there used to be blinds on the windows facing the hall, but the school district had them removed. Now I know why he said it—he'd been hoping for this moment, baiting me into a conversation about the need for privacy. How long had he been waiting for this?

He was still on his knees when I returned.

I resumed my place, slowly spreading my legs, teasing myself with my middle finger.

"Lean forward and pray," I said.

He glanced at the door once, then back at me, his lips parting as if he was about to protest. But the invitation was impossible to deny.

He was sweating, his eyes glazed with lust. He moved toward me.

I stopped him with my foot, pressed firmly against his chest. His will surrendered in whole.

"You want to be good for me, don't you, Mr. Merry?"

He nodded—slow, certain. His hands trembling.

I spread my legs just enough to see him swallow—to see the flush descend upon his face."

This time, he didn't check the door.

Wesley dropped me at the corner of Great Bend and Indian Drive. I walked through the parking lot and into the lobby of the Esmeralda Hotel. Richard Bradberry was an Esmeralda bar regular—I was bait.

Sometimes, I wish I looked more mature. Women are obsessed with youth, but I'm obsessed with age. Maybe that's a luxury baby-faced girls can afford. Either way, there was no chance they'd let me hang around in that bar.

A small café sat at the entrance, so I waited there—not for long. Bradberry rolled in at 11 a.m., right on time, a late-morning starter.

He was handsome—tall and muscular with thick, wavy, platinum-grey hair styled in movie star fashion. I like crème-colored suits on men. Probably not great in the city, but here, with palm trees, sidewalk cafes, and miles of golf courses, crème works well.

He glad-handed his way across the lobby—a real politician of business. Then he spotted me, sitting alone with my book. I was glad he found me worth a greeting—*I did look good*. White knee-high boots and a form fitting brown dress—a perfect complement to him. I'd thought about stuffing my bra—some men love big breasts—but instead, I went for little titties and perv-friendly nipples.

"Good morning" he checked his Rolex, letting it flash for my benefit. "It is still morning, yes?"

"I hope so. I had an early lunch appointment, and if it's afternoon, I've been stood up."

"And he'd be the least intelligent man in this valley." He pulled out a chair "Do you mind?"

"Not at all. To be honest, I was feeling a bit lonely."

He looked at me like I was behind glass, the way he might choose a cut of steak or a lobster—a nice piece of pussy wrapped up for brunch.

"Let's get a couple of drinks over here, Bobby!" He waved a waiter over. There was no hesitation between call and response. "I'll have my usual—and for the lady?"

"I'll have a grapefruit juice—if its fresh squeezed, it not, orange juice is fine."

"You sure you wouldn't like a Greyhound?"

"A bit early for me."

As the waiter hustled off, I straightened my lip gloss.

"If I was old enough to drink, I'd have two. But as it is, I'm fine with the juice."

He sat quietly for a moment—*I thought I lost him. But what could I do? I couldn't risk being carded. Even if the waiter let it slide, it would've looked like I was playing big—a trait I'd find unattractive.*

He wasn't going anywhere.

"Now about your rendezvous," he said. "Is it work-related?"

"Are you committed to know?" I asked.

"Ha! That sounds like one of my lines."

"You have lines?"

"Sweetheart, we all have them."

"Okay, I'll play." I pushed back my hair. "Give me one of your best."

The waiter set our drinks down. Bradberry didn't bother to tip.

"My best line, huh? Well, what am I after? Am I working on a lead?"

"If your lead involves chatting up a young woman sitting alone in a bar, then yes, that's what I'm looking for. Give it your best shot."

He raised his brow. "How old are you?"

"That's a terrible opening—unless you're a bouncer. But I don't find dumb muscle attractive. I'm sure you can do better."

His interest shifted—he'd been seeing me as an easy piece of meat and now he realized there might be something more, a puzzle to play with.

"Ha! I'm sorry." I laughed like a silly little girl and held out my hand. "I'm seventeen, an actress, and I'm here to meet Ron Jacobs—you might know him. He's a producer; lives in the valley."

"You sure had me—dumb muscle." Bradberry flexed his bicep. "I didn't know what the hell was going on, but I'll tell you—I was intrigued. You're good. Real, good." He stood up and grabbed his drink.

"So good I drove you away?"

"No, of course not, I…"

"Be honest—was it Ron, or my age?"

"Neither. I'm meeting a client. I'm a touch late, actually, or else I'd stay and keep you company until your date arrived."

"He's not a date. Not my type. I prefer older men. Good luck."

I guess there's no time like the present to fill you in. Wesley and I drove out here this morning. My mother thinks were doing inventory. Had to be at the shop by six. Wesley's wife is off with her boyfriend—which I can't wait to hear that story, and his daughter's at school.

If he can follow orders and keep his panic attacks in check, Wesley should be securing a room at the El Rancho Mirage. My job is to Venus flytrap this crème-suited Lothario and get him to the hotel. If I'm lucky, he'll show me what he's made of before Wesley turns out the lights.

* * * * *

"Jesus, Wessy. That guy was a fucking creep. I think we might be killing the wrong dude."

Well, thankfully, I didn't ask you. Bradberry is our number one—and what did you expect?

The *'fucking creep'* my mentor was disgusted with was the less-than-honorable Mr. Mike. Marcy hadn't been sure if he still worked here, but he did. He was exactly as she described: a fat, Morrisey-loving border brother with a pompadour and a gold chain bracelet around his wrist—right where she said he'd be—lurking by the pool, drooling over the pre-teen beauties.

"Jesus—Marcy, how did you meet this guy?"

"I never met him."

"Then how do you know he's there?"

"Have you ever slept with an underage girl, Wesley?"

"No, of course not."

"Well, neither have I. But as the one being fucked, I can tell you it's hard to find a safe place to get it on—especially, if you have a wife, a daughter, and a Teacher of the Year plaque in Ocean Park."

She twirled her gum, watching the desert roll by.

"I told you about Merryweather."

"The teacher?"

"Yeah. He was the one who found Mike—don't ask me how, but in the world of online picture swapping and bragging about their underage conquests, this society of trash has a network of like-minded deviants. I wasn't the first little girl Mr. Merry was feeding on. He taught at that school for thirty years, and I was probably well down the line of willing participants."

"How the hell do you work there that long and not get caught?"

"He did. I'm sure you read about it—shot himself in the faculty lot."

"Wait, I did. Mark Merryweather—he was the one you were messing with? Ughhh."

"Ughhh?" She put her hand on my crotch. "Do you think you're any better?"

"I saw his photo in the paper. He wasn't very attractive."

"His cock was." She traced a ten-inch line on the dash. "He was hung like a horse. When you fucked him, you knew it was in you. Besides, he was my coming-out project. "

"But I thought you were the dom. Isn't that what you guys were about?"

"It's about pleasure, Wesley. You think I don't wanna cum?"

"No, but I—"

"He was hung, and I taught him how to hold it up, pretty. I used him—just like I use you. Merryweather brought me out here to fuck."

"So, what am I supposed to do?"

"Mike won't be hard to find. Tell him you're a friend of Johnny Mar—"

"I don't know who that is."

"It doesn't matter—it's just a name he uses. When you shake his hand, palm him $300. He'll set you up with a room."

"No ID, nothing?"

"Yeah, sure. Go to the lobby and register as a sex offender. Ask for their resident deviant. Come on, Boss Man, I'm trying to help you."

"Well, sorry if I'm not a pro at hung cocks, underage fucking, and murder."

"You're going to be a pro at getting your ass kicked if you don't shut up."

I carried a small bag: a change of clothes for Marcy and me, duct tape, a hammer, and my blue plastic cock. I wasn't sure I could summon up that killer vibe without it strapped on, so I figured better rocked up than flaccid.

The room was clean enough. 1970's desert kitsch—palm trees, flamingos, and cigarette burns on the nightstands. I turned down Mike's offer of a free stay if he could watch, closed the blinds, and got things ready. Marcy made me lay out her clothes to make it look like she'd already been there. My job was to wait in the closet, hammer in hand, cock at the ready, and spring out when the time came. I got this.

* * * * *

Bradberry was still in the bar. I ordered a piece of avocado toast and a sparkling water. Wesley's text came through at 11:45:

Room 339. In the back, by the water tower. I'm waiting for the heads up. Mike is gross.

He has no idea. Merryweather talked me into letting that old pool boy go down on me—said it would get us a free room. I took the $300 and let him do it. It was disgusting. It took two weeks to get the scent of cheap, lilac hair grease out of my nose. It wasn't worth it.

Bradberry came out at noon. He looked disappointed, like he was going to walk right past me, wrapped up in his own affairs. I spoke up.

"You look how I feel."

He stopped, started to say my name, then realized I'd never given it.

"Abby—Abby Summers."

"I wish my deal went as good as you look, Miss Summers. What happened to your meeting?"

"He never showed. I got an apology text a few minutes ago, and now I'm trying to figure out what to do."

"What do you mean?"

"Well, my girlfriend went hiking with a guy she met last night, and I need to get back to my hotel."

"Where are you staying?"

"The El Rancho—"

"Mirage?"

"Yeah."

"I'll be glad to drive you. It's on my way."

I could see why the ladies liked him—handsome, not too self-absorbed, and from the look of his pants, he might be carrying something fun up front. I played it easy—vulnerable, not too bold. I thought I might've taken it a step too far at the hotel—most men are afraid of intellect—but it didn't seem to matter.

He put his hand on my thigh. "You must be used to disappointment. How do you deal with it?"

I lifted his hand off my leg. "Do I look like someone who's often turned down?"

"No, I can't say that." He replaced it. "But hopefully, you don't do a lot of turning down either."

"My age doesn't frighten you?"

"You said you were nineteen."

"I said seventeen."

He slid his hand further along my thigh, the back of his little finger brushing against my panties. "I heard eighteen."

I glanced down at his crotch—his pants did little to hide his arousal. I put my hand on his cock. Merryweather had nothing on him. "What do you want, Richard? You gonna take advantage of a lost little girl?"

He pulled the car over and unzipped his pants.

"Not here," I said. "I'm not going down on you on a public street."

"What about your hotel? You said you had a friend. Is she there?"

"No, she's out. Maybe you didn't hear me."

He readjusted his slacks. "I think the blood's gone out of my head. I apologize for forgetting."

He wasn't the only one—the thought of his murder was being slowly overshadowed by my desire to get off. I needed a breath.

"Maybe we should cool it for a minute—grab a drink somewhere." He checked his phone.

"What, a bottle to go? Yeah, that sounds good."

He looked over his shoulder. There was a liquor store on the corner.

"A quick call and a fifth of the Goose—what do you say?"

"Perfect—get ice."

* * * * *

I was watching TV when Marcy's text came through—two words: "heading home."

My heart dropped. My body began to shake, and I felt like I was drifting away from the room. I took off my clothes and walked into the closet with my hammer and rubber cock. They were heavy in my hands.

"Hey, Wessy. I appreciate that wooden handle, but let me give you a heads up: make that first shot count. You get a bunch of blood on that handle, and you're gonna have a problem."

"Your right. I should've gone with a different grip."

"It's okay, just make it count."

"Does it always feel like this? The adrenalin pumping through your body?"

"No, not anymore. You don't want that, you know. That kind of excitement can fuck things up—cool mind, cool body, cruel world. You got this. Killing's easy. But if you get in a bind—which I don't think you

will—I'll step in and wrap it up."

"Thanks, Charles I—"

"Shhhh, they're here."

* * * * *

Bradberry's hand was all over my ass, steering me to the room like a puppet. If he could've speared me with his cock and walked me in like that, he would've.

Thank God Wesley left the door unlocked.

The room wasn't great, but it didn't scream trash either. It was the kind of place clean people go to get dirty.

"If you want to put your jacket down—"

Bradberry pulled me in close, his lips crushing mine. He was stronger than I thought.

"Whoa, easy guy." I gently pushed him away. "Why don't you pour us a couple of drinks while I freshen up."

He shoved me onto the bed. "I don't want you clean."

"I need to pee."

"Goddamn it."

He groaned but gave up easily, grabbing two hygienically wrapped paper cups from the coffee bar. He pulled one of the cellophane covers off and put three fingers inside, holding it like a dick.

"Do you want me to use this? I will, but it's not necessary—I'm shooting blanks."

I pulled it from his hand.

"Is that what condoms are for? I thought it was to inhibit the spread of STI's."

"D's. It's STD's."

He tossed the wrapper in the trash.

"No, it's for infections, not just diseases."

He poured himself a few fingers of vodka—Grey Goose—*a wasted* expense. *All vodka tastes the same.*

"You sure know how to warm up a room," he said.

I got on my knees, undid his pants, and pulled down his briefs, letting his cock bounce off my face. He smelled good, clean, with none of that old man funk. He was also, as promised, more than enough for me—maybe too much.

"I thought you needed to pee."

I put my left hand under his balls, teasing his ass with my middle finger while jerking him into my mouth. I'm a good cocksucker—one of my favorite things—but even so, I could only take him halfway.

"More." He grabbed my head and forced me down, choking me with his cock—deep-fucking my throat. "Come on, Baby." He pushed harder. "Swallow that thing."

I couldn't breathe—panicking, swallowing, and trying to pull away at the same time. He finally released me.

I coughed—drool pouring down my shirt—"I couldn't breathe, you asshole."

He took a big drink and smiled. "Sorry, Baby. I guess I got carried away." He toyed with his cock. "I'll go easy next time."

"I hope so—jerk." I walked into the bathroom. He refilled his cup. "If there's any left can you pour me one?"

"Yeah, sure thing, Babe."

"With ice."

I locked the door behind me.

"Ha! I love hearing that little bitch choking—I'm all rocked up, motherfucker."

I glanced down at my thing. *No, you're not, Charles."*

"You're not." He sounded like a child—an eight-year-old killer with a God complex and a thing for hammers. *"Put on that rubber dick. You fuckers should double team her."*

He's getting the beat-down, buddy. I'm not here to get freaky with him.

I strapped on my cock, tucking my balls through the hole.

"But you'll let him fuck her, right?"

Huh?

"You gonna let him cum first?"

I hadn't thought about it.

"Ha! Whack him right before he shoots—can they cum when they're dead?

How the hell should I know—you're the killer.

"No, you are buddy, and you're getting real good."

What an asshole. I think he bruised my throat.

I pulled the small bindle of foil out of my panties—six 10mg tablets of fine crushed temazepam. My hands were shaking.

I'm worried about Wesley. What if he doesn't hit him hard enough— shit, what if he freezes? What if Bradberry fights back? He's bigger than I thought—stronger too. Wesley said, "old man" and I pictured somebody wobbling around with a cane and a hearing aid. I wasn't thinking of a 70-year-old playboy gym rat packing a python in his pants. He's old, yeah, but not old-old. Shit.

I sat down on the toilet and opened the bindle. A heavy dose is 30mg, and this is double that. I hope it works.

He was naked, lying on top of the comforter when I walked out.

"You're on the counter, Babe."

The remaining bottle of vodka and a cup for me sat on the shelf. I spiked my own drink. He'd been pounding double-shot straights, and he wasn't slowing down. If I kept him near the bed, he'd be sure to finish what was in his cup—and then polish off mine.

I stood at the foot of the bed and took off my clothes. He played with himself as I stripped. He had to be on the blue pill. That thing was rock solid and throbbing. I was looking forward to this.

"Turn around."

I did as he asked.

"Is everything on the menu today?"

I crawled between his legs. "What do you want?"

"You tell me, *Abby*."

He pulled me next to him, turned me onto my back, and spread my legs, crawling over me. "You think I don't know what's happening." The head of his cock hung down between his legs and grazed my cunt. I pushed my hips toward him—I wished he'd stop talking. He reached over and finished his drink. "What's this gonna cost me?"

"Cost you?"

"You must think I'm an idiot, *Abby*."

"Why do you keep saying my name?"

"Am, I?"

"Are you what?" He held me in place with his legs.

"Am I saying your name?"

He reached for my drink, picked it up, and swirled it, starring at the liquid. He held it to his mouth—lips slightly parting....

He was freaking me out. I don't like being on this end of the exchange. I normally hold the reigns, and this old prick was out of my control—come on, guy, drink it.

He tossed it over his shoulder.

Fuck.

"I think you should let me go."

"Do you think I'm an idiot? A pretty young girl hanging around the clubhouse bar, chatting up rich men. I know this hotel, sweetheart. I've been banging little hookers like you for years. If you'd been sitting where I was, you'd have seen the mirror on the wall—the reflection of you juicing up that booze. I should've poured it down your fucking throat."

His weight pressed me into the mattress—his breath, the reek of age, a sun-tanned hand on my throat. I turned my head, stared at the wall, my body limp.

He pushed inside me.

Come on, Wesley. Kill this prick. What the fuck are you waiting for?

Should we go now?

I squeezed the hammer, tightening my grip.

Charles stayed cool—professional.

"No, listen to those bedsprings, man. He ain't drugged. He's bouncing away on that slut."

Each of Bradberry's thrusts felt like a taunt. I couldn't help but think she liked it. I wasn't man enough to do her like that. Maybe I don't have this in me?

"What?"

What if he hurts her?

"If he hurts her? That's the point, fucker. Stop being a bitch—she's got this."

Bradberry's hand clamped around my throat, holding me in place. "Lift that fucking ass up, bitch—I want all of it."

I played dead. If your attacker has nothing to toy with—nothing to satisfy his sick instinct to overpower you, they'll usually let you go. Every bone in my body screamed resist and yet I held still, offered myself to his defeat.

"You're a lousy fuck." He spit in my face. "I'm not paying for a blown-out cunt."

He pulled out of me—relief, for a moment—then he threw my legs back, and slammed into my ass.

"Stop!"

His hand went back to my throat, his thrusts doubling in intensity. I kicked, trying to get away. It was no use.

"This is what happens to tricky little bitches that want to play games."

He was tearing me apart—choking me, unable to breath. I was going out….

Let's go, man—that's it.
"Hold up, Wessy, just hold up… What if he kills her?"
What?
"Look buddy, she's got shit on us—that fucking camera, and she's underage. If we let him kill her, she'd be out of our hair—gone, no hassle."
Are you fucking kidding me? How'd she get out here, genius? You don't think they can tie me to this shit? You're insane.
"Alright, alright, have it your way—but you better get going. I don't hear her breathing."

I quietly opened the closet door—my 6.5 inches of royal blue, flesh-like cock leading the way. He was on top of her, grunting and panting as he came.
I got this.
She wasn't moving.
I held the hammer high—Charles in my head. *"Hit him hard."*
He pulled out of her—her unconscious body callously left behind. Unknowingly, he turned toward me. "Wesley?"
For a moment, I felt pity. The look on his face was so clueless, so childlike.
"What the hell are you doing here?"
My first blow caught him square in the eye, the head of the hammer hanging for a second in the soft flesh. I freed it and swung again. He raised his hands—a weak attempt to protect his face. Useless.
The second hit landed with a solid crack, breaking finger bones and splitting his brow. The next was wilder, catching him above the right temple. He dropped his guard and fell to his knees.
My fourth shot was clean and well-placed, just above the base of the

skull. He collapsed—out for the count—but I kept the hammer at work.

I don't remember how many swings I took—it's hard to keep count when you get swept up in the fun. Later, I read it was somewhere close to fifty. I stopped when my arm got tired.

I know some people dehumanize their targets before they kill, but Bradberry remained, to me, a man—a face, a name, a history, the works, until the life drained from him and into me.

Now I felt nothing—no connection, no compassion. He was just flesh on the floor.

I took off my dick and tossed it onto the chair.

Marcy sat on the bed, her neck bruised, bloodshot eyes staring at nothing. She retched, vomit spilling onto her legs.

An instinct stirred in me to hold her—she was, after all, barely more than a child, but as I moved toward her, it turned to disgust. I despise weakness in women—my mortality reflected in their tears.

I walked over to the sink and washed my hands. I hated her in that moment and wondered if I'd ever care for her again.

Maybe Charles was right. I should've let him kill her.

OUR GAY SAVIOUR

There was no hiding Marcy's injury. We needed a story—a villain, a hero, and above all, an explanation. I pulled into a rest stop and braced myself.

She clenched her fist. "You sure you want me to hit you?"

Her defeated state hadn't lasted long. One moment, she was out of it; the next, she was packing her bag and chatting me up as if nothing happened. I liked her better this way—almost normal.

"No, I don't *want you* to hit me—just do it, right in the fucking—"

Wham!

She connected. The girl could punch. I was instantly swollen—incapable of seeing out of my right eye.

"Goddamn it, Marcy. I wasn't ready. My eye's gone!"

"Quit crying. It's in there—I can see it from here."

That's not funny, Charles. I'm fucking hurt, man.

She was holding her wrist—not like she was injured, but as if she was seeing that weapon for the first time.

I checked myself for blood.

"I couldn't stop him. If it wasn't for you, I'd be dead."

"If it wasn't for me, you wouldn't be here."

"Bullshit, Wesley. This was my idea." She placed a hand on my shoulder. "Will you hold me?"

The disgust of earlier had faded. I put my arms around her, and she rested her head against my shoulder. I hadn't held a woman in years. I strained to remember—Rachel, maybe five years ago. One of those little-girl-and-daddy hugs before she grew up on me. We used to be close. Paula's venomous words had yet to sink in, and she was still mine. I guess Paula finally broke through though. Rachel's turned against me.

"Wesley?"

"Yes?"

"I'm going to kiss you." Marcy pressed against my lips—soft and sweet.

I kissed her back in kind—gentle, without any innuendo behind it.

She kissed me again—lighter this time, then pulled away.

"I'm always in charge, Wesley. It's a game—tough talk, begging and pleading, but it's not real. It's a fantasy—harmless."

Harmless. The word lingered. I thought of her urine in my mouth, her threats of putting me in jail. Bradberry, his brains scattered on a hotel rug. That didn't feel harmless.

"I've never really hurt anyone," she said. "I'm not a bad girl."

No, she wasn't bad—not at all, ey?

It was still early. We'd be home before 3:00.

"Marcy! Oh my God!"

She pulled her daughter into the house—Marcy's father, ran from the back into the living room. The walls plastered with portraits of Jesus, and Father Hezekiah.

"I'm okay, Mom—Mr. Wallace…"

Her father turned on me—livid before my interjection.

"It was a homeless man, sir—probably unstable. She went out to the trash and then…"

"I wasn't doing anything wrong—"

"Of course you weren't, dear." Her mother was nothing short of a Grant Wood painting—a modest black dress, hair in a bun, no-makeup, wire-rimmed glasses—gothic. She dressed as if she were eighty, but she couldn't have been more than late thirties.

"If it wasn't for Mr. Wallace."

Marcy played her part well—almost too well. Her quivering lips were perfectly staged. Sometimes I forget she's a liar—the best I've ever seen.

"Your daughter was taking out the trash and she was attacked."

"Oh, my God."

"I'm okay mom."

"We need to get you checked out." Her mother pulled a grey sweater from the coat rack.

"That'd be a good idea, kid." I put my hand on Marcy's shoulder—*paternally, she was as old as my daughter.*

Her father's eyes zeroed to my offending member—she was, after all, a young female, and in his strict beliefs, my hand on her shoulder was akin to rape. With slight mistrust he surveyed my injured eye—searching for anything out of step.

"Are you okay?" he asked.

I touched the cheekbone below. *Marcy had pounded me—hard.* "Yeah, I'm okay. He got in a lucky shot, I guess." I smiled. "I think we did alright. I'd never been in a fist fight before."

"You did a good job, Wes—right?" Her father shook my hand.

I kept my grip light—limp, but not too limp. He bought it—eye, wrist, and lisp.

"It's Wesley, yes. I wish it didn't happen at all, but we did okay. That daughter of yours is pretty darn scrappy."

Her father laughed.

"Bill." Her mother, impatiently waiting, "I'd feel better if we got her checked out."

"He had her pretty darn good. I—"

"Did they arrest him?" Marcy's father cared more for justice than comfort. "We want to press full charges."

"No—he ran for it, and I'm sorry, but I was more concerned with Marcy than going after him."

Her mom hugged me—I winced.

"You're a good man, Mr. Wallace. Thank you."

I left Marcy in their God-fearing hands and drove to the shop.

I parked in the alley behind the store. I'm not sure why, but I didn't want anyone to see my car. Ridiculous—I should be establishing an alibi.

"Maybe you wanna get caught?"

That's crazy, Charles.

"Is it? Then why are you hiding your car?"

Not everything has a fucking purpose.

"Oh, look at the language on you—two bodies in, and you're already talking like a cold-blooded killer. Ha!"

There was dried blood on the ground—*I hate the homeless.*

"I bet that faggot Waddell would have something to say about that."

Yeah, and what would he say to you, huh? Wait, I can hear him now: I find it extremely troubling that a neurotypical male is establishing a romantic relationship with a person who lives with Down syndrome. Ha!

"She's a saint you asshole!"

Okay, calm down.

My phone was ringing. It was my mother. *She never calls my cell— only the landline.*

"Mom?"

"Bradberry has been murdered."

"What? What the hell are you talking about?"

"It's on the news—turn it on."

"Mom, I'm at the shop. What are you talking about? I just spoke with him."

"He was murdered. Oh my God, Wesley—I'm terrified."

"Mom?"

She hung up.

Shit.

"Ha! News travels fast, huh? I bet he's still bleeding."

"He's dead."

"You better hope so, champ. Did you check his pulse?"

I hadn't.

I went inside and pulled up the Palm Desert news on my computer. A breaking bulletin filled the screen—an attractive newswoman stood on a garden path outside room 339 at the El Mirage hotel. The scene was chaos—cops, bright lights, and cameras. I turned it up.

"...Authorities are investigating the death of a prominent local businessman discovered in a room at the El Rancho Mirage Hotel this afternoon. The victim, whose identity is being withheld pending notification of family, was found deceased by hotel staff following reports of a disturbance in the area."

"Shit, there's Mike."

The pompadoured fat man was in a wide shot talking to the police. He was animated—looked agitated, and if I didn't know better, guilty.

"Don't trip, buddy. What's he got? Nothing. That motherfucker is shitting his pants right now. Could you imagine?"

Charles was right. That Morrisey loving pedo doesn't want anything to do with me, or Bradberry—guaranteed. He's trying to keep his ass out of the pot.

Charles broke into a song, off-key and fruity. *"Hotel girl in a coma, I know. I know, it's really serious!"*

He had a lousy voice. *You're no crooner, Baby.*

"Fuck you, Wessy."

"...Details surrounding the incident remain scarce. Local law enforcement officials have confirmed that foul play is suspected, but they have not disclosed the cause of death. Police are urging anyone with information to come forward as they continue to investigate what

they are calling a "high-priority case."

I called my mother back—voicemail. The impersonal computer voice with an Indian dialect repeated her phone number.

I called again—the same.

My phone rang. It was her.

"Wesley." Her voice had a pleading tone that sickened me. "Is it you?"

"Yeah, of course."

"Did you see it?"

"I did, but what makes you think that's Mr. Bradberry? No names were given."

"He called me."

"When?"

"We had an appointment today. He said he was stopping by the El Mirage."

"He couldn't have called you." *Shit—I gotta calm down.*

"Dear?"

Ugh, her sentimental tone was revolting. "I don't understand. He called you, after he died?"

Marcy didn't tell me he used the phone.

"I told you we should've let that bitch die."

"Shut up."

"Wesley, what are you talking about?"

"When did he call you?"

"He didn't show up to our appointment. I called his office, and they said they hadn't heard from him since this morning. When I saw the news, I knew it was him. I called the police."

"About what? Why would you call?"

"Reel it in, Wessy—you're crossing the line."

Charles was right. One, two, three, breathe... "I'm sorry, mom—I guess this just has me confused and scared. I can't imagine this happening."

"I know, dear. I know how much you liked him."

Okay, now I am getting paranoid. Why the fuck is she being nice to me? And no—I've never liked that asshole, and she had to know that.

"Come on, champ. Tighten it up. Let her talk."

"I don't know how I knew it, Wesley. Call it a hunch, but I had a feeling that it was him. I talked to a detective and he confirmed—oh Wesley, it could've been me."

Theres no way she thinks I'm involved. "I'm sorry, mom. You must be terrified."

"I'm coming there."

"Where?"

"To our house—your house. I want to be with you and Paula and Rachel. I want to be with my family."

Give me a break. One dead asshole and now she needs us. Maybe she forgot she was one loan doc away from kicking us out. Never thought I'd say this, but I prefer her wicked old self.

"Do you want me to come get you?"

"No, I called a service. I'll be there in a few hours."

Fuck. Could this get any worse?

"Ha! Don't be a bitch, Wessy. This is good man. The pot's boiling, the meat's cooking—feel it, feel it in your hide, the thrill of it all. I love this shit. The crazier, the better!"

"Please be safe, mom. I love you."

"I love you too, dear."

I don't know what was harder—me telling her I loved her, or having to listen to her say it to me.

How the hell did it get dark? I must've sat here for hours. Doing what? The news clip was on repeat. How many times had I heard it?

I locked up and went out the back. As I stepped outside, a harsh flashlight beam lit my face.

"Mr. Wallace?"

"Yes?"

It was one of Ocean Park's finest—a street cop on patrol.

"We wanted to talk to you about the attack."

Are you fucking kidding me? How the hell did they finger me?

"I've been here all day—I wasn't in the desert."

"Excuse me?"

There was nowhere to run. The alley had one way in and one way out. *Where the fuck was Charles? What the fuck do I do?* A loose security bulb flickered in time with my heart—jagged, uneven bursts of light.

"I didn't kill him."

"Kill?"

"Bradberry. I didn't kill him."

He was looking at me like I was crazy—*any second now, his hand is reaching for that gun.*

"Bradberry…"

"Wessy! Are you fucking me? Shut your fucking mouth!"

Goddamn it, Charles, where the hell were you?

"I was busy. You fucking snitch."

Another flashlight swung into the alley as his partner rounded the corner—black boots grinding on loose gravel.

"Hey, Tracey. Looks like he locked up and went home. Oh, there you are."

"He didn't kill him, Bob."

"I sure as hell hope not."

The officers laughed—no cuffs, no guns drawn.

"Although," Bob added with a smile, "might've lightened our workload if you had, eh, Trace?"

The disconnection trickled in, like an IV of nitrous. I floated as I spoke.

"I'm sorry—what do you want?"

"Marcy Barrett," the first officer said. "She was attacked earlier today."

"Oh my, God." I snapped back into reality. "You scared the hell out of me."

"Who's Bradberry?"

"Maybe you're the one that needs killing, Wessy. You gotta up your game—you almost threw us away for a fucking nothing."

"He's our realtor. He was murdered today."

"And you thought we thought you did it? Why's that?"

They stared at me, sizing me up against some invisible checklist.

"My mother."

"Does she think you did it?"

"God, no. Do I look like a killer?"

I didn't. I looked like a man who sold women's shoes. There was no grit on my surface. I was cue-ball smooth.

"My mother's got me so freaked out—she thinks they're after her."

"I guess it runs in the family."

Again, with the laughter. I came up clean in their eyes.

Officer Bob took the lead. "You want to tell us about today?"

"Yeah, I… uh…"

A call came across the radio—squawking, beeping, static, and a voice I knew too well.

"You boys in the alley?"

"Yeah, we're around back, detective."

As if this day couldn't get any crazier. I felt his fucking cock round the corner before he did.

"What's up, killer?" His grin was all teeth. "I hear you're after my job."

"Hey, Tony."

DRINKING WITH THE FUZZ

What a prick. He walks onto the scene and makes sure everyone knows who the big dick is.

"Why don't you pull the cruiser around and get a light back here."

"Sure thing, T."

Officer Tracey fell right in line—dick number two, off to get the car and put some light on the scene.

Tony glanced at Bob's empty notebook. "You guys get anything or uh…"

"Not yet, detective. We basically just arrived before you did. There wasn't a sign of struggle out front, so we figured it went down back here. Isn't that right, Mr. Wallace?"

"Yes, she was taking out the trash."

I hadn't thought it would go this far. I figured the story stopped at Marcy's parents. Now I got these assholes poking around.

The cruiser pulled into the alley—it's headlights washing out the scene. Tony was hands on. "Hey, new guy! Cock it sideways for the reflection—are you fucking kidding me—I can't see myself think."

He noticed my eye.

"Jesus Christ, Wes." He held my chin as if he was positioning me for a kiss. "That's some shiner. You were lucky that's all you got. Some of these fucking animals carry blades."

He turned to Bob.

"Remember that piece of shit at the carwash?"

"How could I forget?"

He looked back at me, put his hand on my shoulder.

"We went in thinking it was a random drunk-a-thon—pepper spray and a night-stick, and that motherfucker caught me in the stomach before I knew what hit me."

"What'd you get on that, Tone."

"Seventeen fucking staples—" He ran his thumb across his stomach, tracing the cut. "Seven-fucking-teen. You're lucky, Wes. Now tell me, what happened here?"

"Well, my girl came out to toss the trash—"

"Marcy?"

"Yeah, Marcy."

"We saw her—cute little thing."

What, he's gonna fuck her now too?

"I'll tell you, Wes. The family were sure grateful you were here. I felt proud knowing you."

Proud of me?

I wasn't sure how to reply. "I guess I did what anybody would."

"No. You know that ain't true." His tone softened. "I misjudged you, buddy. Bravery goes a long way with us."

"Goddamn right, T. If more people like Mr. Wallace stood up—it'd be a better place."

Mr. Wallace?

A wicked grin appeared on Tony's face—"But don't go taking that as an excuse to run wild, Wes. We don't need a shoe-selling vigilante around here."

His slight to my ego brought laughter from the boys.

I wanted to step up, tell them about Bradberry—how his eye dangled on his cheek as he begged under my hammer.

"Stow it, Wessy. They're buying your bullshit, and he's fucking your *wife. You wanna brag, do it later—I'll listen."*

I reined it in.

Tony turned his attention to the "crime scene."

"So how'd it go down?" he kicked at an empty box. "Where was Marcy? Did this piece of shit have her on the ground or what?"

I played it out—a stage show, to make them believe.

"He had her right here, against these boxes. I grabbed him by the hair and pulled him back. I guess that's when he hit me. He ran off after that."

"Could you give us a description?"

"No."

"Was he white, black—tall, big guy?"

"I don't know. I guess he was white, but you know how they get when they've been out in the sun, sleeping in the dirt—I'm sorry. I just don't know. I wasn't really paying attention. It happened too fast."

"That's alright, Wes. You took care of business."

Bob swept the ground with his light.

"Looks like we got some dried blood here."

"Opossum."

"Huh?"

"I hit an opossum with the car. I think it's still in the bin if you wanna take a look."

"Oh, fuck no—those are some ugly little fuckers."

Officers Tracy and Bob took off, leaving me alone with Tony.

If you stripped down our history, he wasn't half bad. Back in school, I admired guys like him—jocks that knew their way around the girls. It would've been a badge of honor to be part of that crowd....

"Dude, you don't want to be friends with no cop."

I know, but...

"Besides, it's just fucking weird. Sucking your friend's dick ain't cool."

The thought made me gag.

"Hey, Wes. You wanna go over to Rocco's and get a drink."

"Yeah, sure. I'd like that."

"Consider yourself warned, Wessy."

Four years of pushing shoes on this block, and plenty of nights I could've used a calm-me-down beverage after work. But I've never crossed this street before. I'm not really a dive-bar kind of guy.

We walked through a green-vinyl upholstered door. It was dark, smelled like sour beer, and Christmas lights were strung across the ceiling. I liked it. Maybe it was the colors or the womb-like closeness of the walls—that protective feeling of a hidden space—but I was sorry I'd never been here before. Tony walked in like he owned the place. It wasn't crowded, but there were a few barflies hanging around. I recognized the local mailman—who I knew was a drunk, the guy who ran the sandwich shop on the corner—who I assumed was a drunk, and the mechanic from Louie's place—whose fuck-up on my brake job now makes sense.

We got a couple of brews and took a table next to the jukebox—the same song playing over and over—*"By the time I get to Phoenix she'll be rising...."*

"I didn't know she was married, Wes."

"Who?"

"Your wife. I didn't know she was married."

Christ, I didn't know this was gonna be one of those kinds of talks. I wasn't prepared for this.

"It's alright."

"No, it isn't." He put his hand on his chin—*a perfect cleft.* "And then, when I found out, she said you were into that kind of thing..." He paused, genuinely concerned, and took a drink. "Are you? Do you like doing that?" He held up two fingers, and the barmaid nodded her reply. "If you don't want to get into it, it's okay—I understand, man"

"No, I'm alright." I peeled the label off my beer and ran my fingers across the gum under the table—*more pieces than I expected.* "It's just… it's kinda a weird thing to talk about, huh."

He laughed and downed his drink. I nursed mine. *He was cool.*

"I remember my buddy asking me if I jerked off—shit, I was about sixteen at the time, and it freaked me out. That was a secret, man. You didn't talk about shit like that."

The barmaid dropped two more on our table. I made eye contact, and without a word, she got the message that I didn't want another.

"Nowadays, joking about jerking off, banging hookers, and getting it on is just guy talk." He guzzled his brew. "But not the creepy shit—you can't just blurt out that you sucked some guys cock after he fucked your wife, eh?"

"I suppose not."

"Are you gay, Wes?"

You know the answer—is it worth explaining again?

"I don't got a problem if you are—especially in these days—we gotta guy at the station that's a cocksucker—a fucking sergeant. I just wondered, I guess. Hey, if you're doing the sucking, or letting somebody suck it, it's the same thing right?"

He laughed and finished his beer, held up two fingers, and put his eyes on the bottle I'd yet to touch. I pushed it in his direction.

"I'm not attracted to men if that's what you're asking. I like women."

"You like Marcy don't you?"

"What?"

"Ha! You do know I'm a cop right?" He chugged my beer. "Perpetrators are pretty easy to spot. I asked if you were gay, and you answered real casual-like—it wasn't a charged response, no big deal—and honest. I believe you—a straight man who sucks the occasional dick. I dig it. But when I said something about Marcy, emotionally you flared—protested hard. What's that fucking line?"

"Shakespeare, the guilty doth protest too much, methinks."

"Ha!" He held up his bottle for a toast. I nodded in his direction.

"You're a quick little fucker, Wes." He eyed the barmaid. "Also... you called her 'your girl.' I caught that."

He was smarter than I thought.

He had something in his nose—*please, the napkin, use the napkin.* He didn't—*ughhh.*

"And maybe you'll feel good about this, but I caught that vibe off her too."

"Really? Do you think her parents noticed—not like anything's going on or anything."

"No. They didn't pick up on it, and you're uh... obsession is safe with me. Her mom and dad were more concerned with whether I went to church that day."

The barmaid delivered him another, and for me, a smile. He was half-way through the beer before she returned to her station.

"So, you just do what you do with your wife because you like it— like a fetish or something?"

"Yeah, I guess you could say that. I can't please her, so I guess that's my way to keep her close."

He understood that. Maybe he had cared about his wife and kids. Maybe he didn't want them to leave.

He reached across the table put his hand over mine.

"I'm sorry I talked to you the way I did. I was just getting into the scene, you know?"

"Yeah, I know. I played my part, huh?"

"Ha! You sure did—and if you do go gay, you're quite the cocksucker."

Somewhere after his sixth beer, he ordered a bourbon back and had three more of those. He was in no shape to drive.

I propped him up near the door and brought my car around. If this was out of the regular, the barmaid didn't protest. She must be used to this.

I wonder what the rule is on that—still breathing, non-combative, and not breaking up the place, they're good to go? Who knows?

I helped him into the passenger seat and buckled him in.

"I fucking hate these things." He pulled the belt slack and looped it around his neck. "We don't need it, you know, if they pull us over, I'll just fucking flash this—" he yanked his gun from the holster. "Bam, Bam, Bam!"

"Hey!"

"It's okay—you drive, I'll shoot."

"Why don't you put it up, Tony."

"Or better yet, why don't you hand it to us? We'll put it up."

"Be quiet, Charles. I got this."

"Charles? Who the fuck is, Charles?" Tony loosened the belt and tapped the gun against his head. "I'm the man in charge, motherfucker. I ain't Charles!"

He one-eyed me for double-visions sake. "You do got it, Wes. Don't you?"

"Yeah, Tony. I got it."

He holstered the gun and puked out the window.

MOTHER'S DAY

My mother arrived that Saturday night and by Wednesday morning it was as if she'd been there all along.

"Not my mother, I know you're not talking about her, Wessy. You know she sold me, right?"

Yeah. I was sorry to hear that, Charles.

"It was a real bad thing she'd done, but I felt like I was helping out—contributing to the family."

Did you ever forgive her?

"That's not my job. I don't forgive anybody for anything. It's above my paygrade. What about you?"

I don't think I've been hurt enough to forgive. I take a more pragmatic approach to life. I'll leave the spirit to you, Charles. I'll stick with the flesh.

There was a strange pause in my head, a moment of inner doubt without thought—he was waiting.

"Hey, can I talk to you about something?"

Sure.

"That Debbie thing really fucked me up."

What do you mean?

"Do you think I'm damaged for good? I used to think that there was no changing me—the evil done and all that. I read if a kid doesn't bond

with his mother—or if he suffers emotional trauma in his early years, that he's fucked for life—and I was okay with that, it's a shit hand to be dealt, but lots of people get shit hands. And then, after you stopped me, sent me in the right direction, and Debbie and I got to make love, it felt like I could be something more."

Don't go soft on me, Charles.

"You little fucker. I open up and you give me that?"

"Look, I don't mean to be selfish here, but I need you. I got things I have to wrap up. Do I think you can change, become a new man? Of course I do. I can see it in you. But let's take care of business and then get you on your way, deal?

"Deal."

Rachel was on the sofa, cuddled up next to her grandmother. *I felt sick—thinking of that old hags dusty breath in my daughter's face.* When I walked in, they smiled.

"Well, don't you two look comfy."

Rachel snuggled closer and closed her eyes—*all Paula's beauty, and hopefully, half her intent.* My mother stroked her hair.

"Remember when I used to hold you, Wesley?"

No, I didn't. I can't remember her ever showing me affection. My father used to say, 'a roof over your head, a warm meal in your stomach—that, son, is our love.' Great job, Ambrose. I never asked for more, nor did I care that it wasn't delivered.

I lied. "I do, mom."

They had a nice little fire burning on the grate.

"Have you seen your mother, Rachel?"

"She said she was going to the store, but that was hours ago. Want me to call her?"

I threw another log on the fire.

"No. I've got to get to work."

"How's it going at the store, dear?"

I choked down the bile. I don't know what nice-bug crawled up my mother's ass, but I didn't like it.

"It's actually going pretty good, Mom. I took out an ad, and the response has been tremendous."

"And how's that little girl—doing better?"

"Yeah, Marcy? She's doing alright. Took a few days off, but now she's back at it."

Rachel scooted away from her grandmother and straightened her dress.

"I used to have math with her."

"Really?"

"Yeah, I thought I told you that."

"No. She told me she knew you, but she never mentioned a class."

Rachel checked her phone, looked up at me, and sent whoever it was to voicemail. "I didn't hang with her or anything."

"Hang?"

"It's kid talk, mom. They didn't go around together."

"Oh."

"She didn't go around with anybody. She used to get bullied a bit, but it didn't last. She never reacted, and if they don't react, it's no fun."

"Well, I sure hope you're not bullying anyone. It sounds like you know the score."

"Come on, Dad."

My mother pinched Rachel's cheek.

"Does this look like a bully, Wesley?"

She looks like her mother.

Marcy's mom hovered in the shop, visible through the front glass. She didn't want Marcy back at work—too dangerous—but Marcy insisted. The compromise? Mrs. Barret stuck around until I arrived.

"What the fuck is this, Mother's Day?"

Lighten up, Charles, you know why she's here.

"Tell her you're Satan—see what she says."

Do you need attention?

"Maybe I do. When was the last time you thought about me—my life."

Are you kidding? I just got you laid.

"Check the calendar, Wessy. My cock's starving."

He was right. I hadn't written in weeks. With him in my head, I figured I didn't need to put him on paper. I turned the rear-view mirror to face me.

"I'm sorry, buddy. How about I leave work early, get some time in?"

I accepted his non-reply as a yes.

"Good morning, Mrs. Barrett."

She was wearing the same stark-black dress as the other day—and probably the day before that. Either she had a closet full of them, or she didn't spill.

She looked at me as if I was trespassing in my own shop.

I hit her with a line of scripture—*Charles' suggestion.*

"If anyone does not abide in me, he is thrown away like a branch and withers; and the branches are gathered, thrown into the fire, and burned. John 15:6"

"You've been reading the good word, Mr. Wallace. How does this suit you? 'For if we go on sinning deliberately after receiving the knowledge of the truth, there no longer remains a sacrifice for sins, but a fearful expectation of judgment...'"

I had no idea what she was talking about, but between the lines, it sounded like a warning against returning to my "gay" ways.

"Yes, a powerful piece, Mrs. Barret. How's everything going?"

"My stubborn daughter is in the back with the vacuum, and I'm waiting to be off to church."

It was Wednesday. I had no idea they praised God during the middle of the week.

"Then you may, without worry, leave her under my watch—not a hair shall be harmed. Ha!"

She didn't laugh. To her, my heroics were a lucky strike. She was waiting for God to cast me into the pit.

She said her goodbyes to Marcy, and then she tightened her bonnet and stepped toward the exit.

"And remember, Mr. Wallace, you live in God's grace. After your battle with Satan this week, I'm sure you're in His favor. But the law is not laid down for the just—'but for the lawless and disobedient, for the ungodly and sinners, for murderers, and the sexually immoral, men who practice homosexuality, and whatever else is contrary to sound doctrine.'"

"Thank you Mrs. Barrett—have a blessed day."

She closed the front door like she was leaving a temple, careful not to disturb prayer.

Marcy looked great—able to transcend the filth of being human.

What the hell did her mother say about the sexually immoral? I'd like a piece of that.

Marcy read my mind.

"Can I see you in the back room, Boss Man?"

"Yes, dear."

I lapped at her heels—eager and willing.

Marcy perched on my desk, stunning in a dark grey dress. Modest by most standards, scandalous by her mother's. She hitched it up, and spread her legs—white knee socks, no panties.

"Let me lock the front door."

"No."

"No?"

"No. We don't need it locked. Give Baby a sweet little kiss."

I knelt before her—*my princess, master, confidant.* A white cotton string clung to her vagina like a loose thread. She was menstruating.

"Don't be a baby, Wesley. Kiss it real sweet."

I did as she asked—a quick, fatherly peck. As I pulled away, she grabbed my head and pushed me against it.

"Lick it, you worthless piece of shit." She pulled my hair. "Get that fucking tongue out and clean it."

The taste was metallic. Medicinal.

"Do I disgust you, Boss Man?"

"No, dear."

"Then why the fuck aren't you grateful." She shoved me away. "Be glad I don't feel like cumming."

She hopped off the desk, swiping a pile of papers to the floor, and led me into the showroom. She picked up a black leather pump—stiletto heel.

"Wesley, I'm bored."

"Bored? You still have a bruise on your neck."

She ran her finger across it. "Yeah, but I didn't get to do anything."

"What do you mean?"

"You know what I mean. Killing. I didn't get to kill anybody."

She was terrifying.

Have you ever heard the story about the child and the snake? The child found it—beautiful, docile—and held it close, even slept with it. Then they found out it was poisonous—a deadly viper.

The serpents colors had just appeared on Marcy—a bright red band around her neck. And I had been kneeling at her feet.

"I want to take a shot at it, Wesley. I want to kill somebody. What about that asshole that's sleeping with your wife? Can we do him?"

"Are you fucking crazy?"

"Actually, she isn't. I have an idea."

Charles voice was loud, wandering rude, into the center of the conversation—overriding my power to keep him at bay.

"Charles says he might have something."

"Who the fuck is Charles—the voice in your head?"

"Yeah, you met him." *She didn't run. Didn't flinch. She just said she wanted to kill someone so*—"Can I let him out?"

"Out?"

She looked around the room as if he was hiding in a closet.

"Get the dick, Wes. Where is it?"

"He wants the plastic cock. Where'd you put it?"

"You were the last one who had it. What'd you do with it?"

In all the excitement I forgot. Where the hell was that thing? Jesus, I hope I didn't leave it behind.

"Did you wear it out of the hotel?"

"I…I don't know."

"What do you mean you don't know?"

"Fuck, Marcy—he almost killed you. He was bleeding all over the place—I was trying not to step in it. How the fuck am I gonna remember something like that?"

"Did you take it off? You didn't drive home with it on did you?"

"I need that dick, Wessy."

"Are you kidding, Charles? Is it a magic dick or something? Can't you come out without it?"

"No, I can't."

She moved away from me. "What are you talking about?"

"It's him, he says he needs it. Let me think."

She stood by the counter as I replayed the hotel scene in my head; *Marcy lying motionless on the bed, Bradberry cowering at my feet, begging. The hammer clenched in my hand. The cock—waving in front of me like a standard in battle. I was near the window, the curtain torn. Fuck….*

"I left it on the chair."

"Are you fucking kidding me? You're an idiot."

"I know. I'm sorry. Can the cops get prints off that thing?"

"I don't know. Look it up."

She walked back into my office, standing over my desk chair like a teacher about to hammer an unruly student.

I sat down and started typing but stopped.

"You know, if they check my searches, they'll find this—and don't tell me to delete. I've seen those shows. Those guys always get caught: 'How do you cut up a body,' 'What about decomposition.' Those cops can trace this shit."

In disgust, she kicked my chair, walked across the room, and sat down.

"Was it soft or porous?" she picked up her phone. "Do you remember?"

"It was life-like."

"So, porous, right?"

"Yeah, I guess so."

I wasn't sure. I don't think it had pores, but it was kinda fuzzy. Charles, do you remember if it had pores?

"I'd like to forget this fucking faggot search you two morons are getting into. 'We found his prints on a dildo' shit—even if they did, they'd never say that in court."

Marcy raised an eyebrow. "Have you ever been arrested, Wesley."

"Yeah, but it was… "

"Never mind. Don't worry about it. They're not getting your prints off a rubber cock."

"See!"

"What's Charles want to do?"

"Tell her to get me a new dick. I can't operate under these small circumstances."

"He wants a new dick."

"What if I promise? Will that do it?"

What do you say, sport? She'll get you another one.

My grip on reality loosened, the edges of my mind split. A tremor shot through me, and then—Charles.

"What's up, sugar tits. Let me see that little clam."

"Charles, stay focused." I was now the voice in his head.

Yeah, yeah. I got it man.

He turned to Marcy. "You see, bitch, that fucking cop is a drunk. He leaves his piece out—a .38. Real fun little popper. Next time he goes down, I grab it, and we take a walk."

"Where do you wanna go?"

"Hookers or bums, Baby. Nobody gives a fuck about… wait. What about that big ol' scar on his stomach? That motherfucker hates street trash—can't stand 'em."

"Who can't?"

"Tony, the pig. The wife-fucker. Let's drop a couple street rats with his piece—shoot it, clean it, stick it back in his sock. I'm a fucking genius, man. You want excitement? Put a couple slugs into a piece of human waste. Not only will you be entertained, you'll be doing a service to the community."

He moved toward her, slipping his arm around her waist and pulling her close.

"I was gonna let that sunburned prick kill you, and that bitch Wesley saved your ass. Remember that next time you want him licking that bloody cooze."

He slapped her, walked into the bathroom, yanked down my pants, and laughed at my cock.

"Didn't your mother ever tell you to sit down when you piss."

I came back to reality with my pants around my ankles, and my ass on the cold porcelain seat.

CALL ME UMA

It was an attempt to be nice. My mother likes cocoa, so I was in the kitchen cooking her favorite: cinnamon, a little cayenne... *is that the correct term, cooking?*

"Who gives a fuck?"

I was just wondering

"If you spit in it and stir it in vigorous, you're whisking. If you keep it nice, you're cooking."

Oh, you're in a mood today. What happened to that nice boy, the one who was thinking about being better?

"You need to make up your fucking mind—you want it soft, you want it hard. I ain't your fucking lover, Wessy. What'd you used to tell, Rachel—you get what you get, and you don't throw a fit. Look alive punk."

"Hey, Dad."

"Hey, Baby. How's it going?"

She hopped up on the center island—*I couldn't help thinking of Marcy on my desk.*

"That was really brave of you, taking on that homeless guy."

"I'd rather not talk about it."

"Why not?"

"I didn't really do anything."

I poured my mother's cocoa into a cup—*it looked like Charles might have spit in it.*

"I got punched—not much of a hero."

"But you did it."

"Yeah." She watched my eyes as I paused. "I did it."

She leaned over the cup, brought the steam to her face.

"That smells good—you should try a pinch of *hoja santa* to deepen the flavor."

"Your grandmother would deepen my shame if I screwed with her cocoa. Where do you get this shit?"

"I read, Pops. The yard's full of cool plants. Did your father design the garden?"

"I don't know. I didn't know him that well."

"You lived with him."

"I lived in the vicinity of his ego. How about that."

Her phone buzzed. She glanced down, sent it to voicemail.

"You've been doing that a lot lately."

"Tyson."

"I thought you guys were a thing."

"We were."

I set my mother's cocoa on a saucer and handed her a napkin—*old people, they got a fixation with tidiness.*

"Hang on a second, sweetheart. Don't leave." She reached for me—skinny, skeletal hands adorned with black bruises and a set of large diamond rings. "Wesley…"

"I'm sorry, mom. I've got Rachel in the kitchen."

She'd been trying to speak with me since she arrived, but I'd been putting her off. I know she's gonna corner me one day, but until then, I'll keep moving.

Rachel hadn't left. I pulled up a stool. She looked down on me.

"I'm sorry about the other night, Dad. I didn't think I could ever face you again."

"Sweetheart, I appreciate that. Don't worry. Just drop it. It's over."

"Daddy, when Uma was holding me…"

"Uma?"

"Grandma."

"She asked you to call her Uma? That was *my* grandmother's name—what the fuck?"

She stared at me. "I saw the look on your face—the hatred."

"I don't hate my mother, sweetheart."

"Daddy, you can't mention her without stiffening up. I saw it. I wish you'd be honest with me."

I hung quiet for a moment, measuring my words. "I think hate is a little strong—despise would be better."

She laughed, and the tension in the air broke.

"Rachel, I don't know the woman you're hugging. My mother was cold and heartless. A conniving bitch that abused my father, belittled me at every turn, and held security and home over my head as a way to get me to dance."

"Why'd she put you in the hospital?"

"What the hell—where'd you hear that?"

"My mother."

"I should've known. I was having emotional problems. They couldn't deal with me—no, they weren't *willing* to deal with me, so they put me away."

"And your father?"

"What the hell was she telling you?"

"Don't get mad—it didn't work."

"What didn't?"

"I think Mom wanted to turn me against you. She threw out 'loony bin' and 'guilty' as a way to lessen your influence over me, but it didn't work. That night with Tyson changed me. I realized, sitting in the back of your car, sickened and ashamed of myself, that you weren't the bad guy. I'm sorry, Dad."

I didn't know what to say.

"You don't gotta say anything sometimes. You can hold it in, think it over, say it later if it needs to be said—let her lead, remember."

Wow, a voice of reason from you? That's a first.

"Fuck you, Wessy."

She hopped off the counter and gave me a hug.

"I'm your girl, Dad."

"I know, sweetheart. Thank you."

Paula walked into the kitchen, tossed her keys on the counter, and poured herself a glass of wine.

"This looks like a nice little scene."

"Dad showed me how he makes Grandma's cocoa."

"That's nice, dear. Did you see the rings on her fingers? I'm surprised she can lift the cup."

"Ciao, Dad." Rachel kissed my cheek and walked out.

"Ciao?" Paula ruffled my hair. "Your faggotry is rubbing off. Why don't you see if your mother will take me shopping?" She held up her hand. The humble wedding diamond catching the kitchen light and brightening her eyes. "It's time for a new stone."

How the fuck can someone be so blatantly greedy?

"How the fuck have you not noticed? This shit is old news man. That cunt's a human leech, Wesley. Be glad she hasn't killed you."

She's not violent.

"Not yet. But I'll tell you—she keeps getting pumped up with that big ol' dick and things are gonna change—you're out, he's in."

I washed out the pan and dried my hands. Paula's presence in the room was a heaviness I couldn't shake. Her voice made it worse.

"Tony wants you to come tonight."

"I don't feel like it."

"He knew you'd say that. What the hell did you guys talk about?"

"Nothing—guy stuff."

"Guy stuff? Like he's the guy, and you're the stuff?"

"Fuck you, Paula."

She was laughing as I walked out.

"Hey, Wormsie," her voice trailed me like used tissue stuck to my shoe. "Be ready at seven."

King Kwong's was an outdoor adventure store on Pine, just like Charles said. Fishing gear and tents lined the aisles, fluorescent lights struggling to mimic the outdoor sun. The air smelled of plastic and broken promise—*Wesley, I think we'll go camping this summer. No Ambrose, we won't.*

I went to the counter and took a number.

There are two types of personalities—yeah, I know there's more, but for what I'm telling you now, there's the guys that want to be seen, and the ones that don't. I'm glad I fall into the latter category. I've met short men who seemed almost resentful when I spoke with them–like they didn't want to be seen with another short man, as if our association would somehow exaggerate their lack of height. It must be hell to be them. These are the ones that start fights, walk around with a chip on their shoulder, and constantly try to prove their manhood. Thankfully, I'm of the other type. I don't mind being small. Small means that you don't see me, I'm not a threat, and I'm not someone you would ever expect to be dangerous.

"How can I help you, sir?"

He was barely of age—a young man, maybe working his first job.

"I need to buy some bullets and maybe, like a bag or something."

"A bag?"

"Yes, something that he could carry it in, or whatever you guys use."

He smiled at me—not unkindly. "I take it you're not a gun enthusiast."

"Oh God, heavens no. It's for my boy. His stepfather bought him a firearm, and I'd like to support the gift."

"Excellent—well, I hope he bought it here."

"Do you need to buy the bullets from the same store that the gun came from?"

"Oh, Wesley, you are a crafty bitch."

"No. What'd he get—a rifle, maybe a shotgun for hunting?"

"It's a pistol."

"Do you know what type?"

"I do." I pulled a scribbled note from my pocket. "It's a Smith and Wesson, .38 police special." I bent down and looked through the glass. "It's like that one—exactly. Maybe he did get it from here."

He unlocked the case and retrieved the gun.

"That's it—same handle and everything."

He held it out to me. I backed away. "No, thank you. I'm not a gun person. To be honest, I didn't like the gift, but I wanted to be in his life."

"Everything alright here, bud?"

A man, unmistakably the boy's father, put his hand on his son's shoulder. I felt jealous.

"Yeah, Dad. This gentleman is looking for some ammo, and maybe a range bag, and…"

"The whole thing. It's for my son—a present."

"There's nothing like shooting. The family that shoots together, stays strong together." The man handed me a flyer. "Would you be interested in one of our tactical programs? We have a class starting this weekend."

If I didn't have previous plans, it looked like fun.

"Thank you. I'll give it to my boy. I'm not sure what he and Greg— that's his stepfather—have on the horizon, but I'll pass it along."

In unison, they thanked me for my business.

It must be nice to work with your father—have shared interests and common goals. My father is good at resilience. Twenty-four years in a coma, hanging on, teasing me with his existence, making me wonder if he's ever going to open his eyes and point me out: "he did it."

I paid cash and walked out with a box of ammunition, a cleaning kit, and a smart little gun bag that I could strap to my chest.

RUDE AWAKENING

My mother tried to talk to me when I got home, but I blew by her on my way to the pool house. I'd promised Charles I'd revisit his life, and I think I owe him that.

I stepped over a pile of cut banana leaves and garden trimmings.

When Bradberry died the work stopped mid-stroke. Good. It was a much larger job than they'd thought. The whole back half of the yard was still untouched. They hadn't even made it to the pool yet. It was still in its unused state—broken tile and a deep end harboring twelve inches of brackish green water. Now that they're out of the picture, I might get that work done. It'd be nice to step out of my office and dive into the deep end.

I guess Bradberry was right about this old shack—not about its usage; it's served me well. But it's in a real state. The roof needs doing, the paint, the windows, the flooring—the whole thing. I guess I didn't notice before. It was a sanctuary—water bugs and all.

I stepped on a small roach and walked inside.

Click, click, click—punch. Click, click, click—punch….

You wanna talk about Guess Who's Coming to Dinner—I'm white as rice, but the last thing her minders expected was a man in charge of all his faculties hopping into bed with their sweet little angel.

"I want you to meet them, Charles."

"Sweetheart."

"I like it when you call me that. I'm your sweetheart."

She squeezed my hand.

"I don't think they're gonna approve of me."

"I approve."

"Yeah, but, they might not think you're capable of understanding."

"I live alone, Charles. I'm a grown-up."

"Don't get mad."

"I'm not mad. I'm big and doing good. There's Mary."

Mary was her minder, a woman from the center who checked in on Debbie bi-weekly. She had a stern, no nonsense look that wasn't softened by the "loving servant," wardrobe she'd adopted—the cuddly teddy bear print on her sweater didn't exactly say, let's get it on.

Mary knocked twice, opened the door, and poked her head in.

"Debbie?

My girl stood with her arms to her side—stiff, antagonistic, defensive. She didn't answer.

"Debbie?"

"I'm with Charles. I like him."

Mary pushed the door open all the way. I rose to greet her.

"Good morning." I held out my hand. "Charles Stinson."

She didn't offer hers. "Good morning, Charles."

Debbie held her place, a dog protecting her yard.

Mary took off her sweater and draped it over a chair—without words, she wanted to show me ownership and familiarity.

"Debbie doesn't usually have company."

"I can have company if I want."

Mary gave me the once-over, weighing me against Debbie's defensive posturing.

"Of course you can. I brought you a gift."

Mary set a small potted plant on the table. She looked at me as she deliberately removed the corpse of the last potted gift that had withered from neglect. I got the message—she owns Debbie, and Debbie can't even take care of a simple house plant. So, what do you think you're gonna do with her?

"I'm grown, Mary."

"Of course you are, dear."

"I'm not a child."

I put my hand on Debbie's arm—a gentle touch, careful not to grab or steer, just reassurance. Mary's eyes tracked every move.

"Where did you two meet, Charles?"

"At the supermarket."

"He had an address on my street. I helped him find it."

Debbie's hands were clenched.

"I'm afraid Debbie's hostility is my fault."

"You can be here. You're my sweetheart."

Mary ignored her. "How so, Charles?"

"I was telling Debbie that our friendship—"

"—you're my sweetheart."

"Yes, I am." *Mary's eyes widened.* "I was telling Debbie that people might have a problem with us being together."

"He can be here, Mary."

"I didn't say he couldn't. You're grown."

"I am." *Debbie smiled and released her tension.*

"Do you work at the supermarket, Charles?"

"No, I don't. I'm sort of retired."

"At your age?"

"We had a family business. It was sold after my father passed. I basically haven't worked since."

I could see my predator's shadow in Mary's eyes. She needed more.

"I haven't had to. Our business was quite successful—a family enterprise, and I'm basically at my leisure."

"Do you mind me asking what business?"

"Not at all. My father was heir to Stinson Steel—I was, and am, last in line."

Now to most people, being heir to a family fortune was attractive, even awe-inspiring—but not to Miss Mary. I'd have been better off playing the part of a sanitation man on the city tit. Money and I said: this motherfucker is out of his mind and looking for kicks—tard fucking.

"Tard fucking? Where do you come up with this shit?"

Wesley, get out.

"No, I won't. Why don't you give her the benefit of the doubt? Look, Charles, I don't care how you slice this. People are gonna think you're trying to take advantage of Debbie—it's only natural."

But what if I tell them what I see in her—her purity and innocence, her inability to hurt others?

"Listen to me, please. Go easy. Don't be paranoid."

But you said she was worried.

"She is, but don't aggravate it."

Okay.

Sometimes a bit of chatter can smooth the way. I'm not as slick as Wesley, or as unimposing, but I can smile and make small talk.

"Debbie says you work at the center. Do you enjoy it?"

"I do. It has its challenges, as do most things, but it's very rewarding."

"I bet it is. One of the things that attracted me to Debbie was her kindness. I'd love to see where she went to school."

"I don't go anymore, Charles. I work at the grocery."

"I'm glad you do."

"Sweetheart. I'm your sweetheart."

"Yes, dear." I took Debbie's hand. "My sweetheart."

Mary checked her watch and begged our pardon. I had the feeling she didn't want to leave us alone, but also that she had no real reason to stay.

I watched from the window as she got into her car. Mary was on the phone before the key hit the ignition.

I waited until she drove away and then I locked the door and pulled the blinds. I didn't want them to take Debbie from me.

"I wish you hadn't been so mad, Baby."

I led Debbie to her bed.

I've lived too many years without her. The world owed me this.

I unbuttoned her blouse and removed it, unfastened her bra. I kissed her neck, then worked my way to her breasts—teasing and sucking. I undid her pants and slid them and her underwear to the ground.

"Ha!"

"What's so funny, Charles?"

I got down on my knees and kissed her stomach.

"I'm laughing at the fucking wig you got down here."

"I don't have a wig."

I gently bit her labia and then pulled away with her hair in my mouth. "If there's a fire, you're gonna go up like a dried weed."

"You're mean."

"No, I'm not—just teasing. Let me clean you up."

She handed me a pair of scissors and an old Bic razor. Looked dull—I didn't want to hurt her.

"You don't have an electric?"

"No, I don't."

"It's okay, Baby."

I grabbed a small waste basket, told her to spread her legs. I trimmed her with the scissors as close as possible, then held up a mirror so she could see.

"How's that?"

"I look like a little girl. Do you like it, Charles?"

I kissed it, light and sweet. "I love it. Hang on."

I took a warm, wet washcloth and softened the hair and skin—I used crème rinse instead of soap. The razor wasn't as dull as it looked. She had a beautiful cunt—thick, with large lips.

I held the mirror up again.

"Do me a favor, Baby. The next time Mary stops by, don't tell her I shaved that little pussy."

"I won't."

"You know she's gonna be back soon."

"She comes on Friday and Tuesday."

"Okay, but don't be surprised if she goes to your work—asks about me."

"You're my sweetheart."

"I know, dear."

Click, click, click—punch. Click, click, click—punch....

I didn't see that coming. Maybe I need a trim.

"Oh, so you do love me, Wessy! Thank you!"

"You asked me to revisit your life, and I did. You, my friend, are a deviant of the utmost—"

"Really? A deviant? You like those big muffs? It looked good shaved... and tasted even better."

"Ha!"

"Oh, oh—you got company, pal."

She'd wandered into the backyard—"Who are you talking to, Wesley?"

"Mom? What are you doing?" Surprise scattered my feelings of resentment, but they quickly returned. "Why are you out here?"

"I wanted to see you, dear."

"Don't call me that. You never did before."

"I know, Wesley. I'm sorry for—"

"Mom, stop it. I don't want to hear that shit."

"I wish you wouldn't talk like that."

"I'm working."

"I know you are, dear. I wanted to see what you were doing."

"You've never given a fuck about me—except when you were getting off on shaming or humiliating. Keeping me small. Is that what you want to do, take a few shots before bedtime?"

The flood of resentment fell true.

"Wesley, please don't."

"Don't what? Say it like it is?"

"You're right. I know you are, but Bradberry's death—"

"Bradberry? Here's some news, mom. I'm glad he's dead."

"Wesley!"

"And you having some fucking change of heart because you can finally see your mortality—and the pile of shit that you've become— does nothing for me."

"Wesley, I'm—"

"Sorry? Is that what you were going to say?"

She began to cry—rusted over tear ducts pumping archaic emotion. I wanted to wipe her face in her pain.

"Get out of here. Go away. Take your remorse with you."

She turned from my door, her cane searching for footing along the pool's edge. "I am sorry, son."

"Don't call me that. I'm evil, remember? A mistake that never should have happened. That's what you told me. I'm evil."

"You are not. You're my son."

"I killed Bradberry, mom."

She stared at me with horror in her eyes.

"I bashed his fucking head in. Now get the fuck out of here."

"No!"

I kicked her—not hard enough to send her down, just enough to betray her footing. She reached for me to steady herself, and I hesitated before pulling my hand away. The earth gave way beneath her, and she fell into the empty pool—nine foot six down, slamming onto the bottom and sliding into the dark green bile with a sickening thud and splash.

"Shit. That escalated quickly."

Stay out of it, Charles—she's mine.

I walked casually to the shallow end and down the steps—the aging concrete crackling beneath my feet. I worked my way to the deep end and knelt near her body.

She was sporadically but slowly breathing.

"You know what a spiritual awakening means, Mother? It means you woke up, and you feel remorse, and you want to set things right. But your awakening didn't do shit for me. I don't give a fuck."

I stood up. The horizon was above my head. A noise came from the house—a window opening. I looked to see, and Rachel was staring down at me.

How long had she been there?

She lifted her phone to her ear.

I sat down on the steps, facing my mother's body.

Oh well. Fuck it.

As she took her last breath, I wandered into the emptiness in her eyes.

BRING OUT YOUR DEAD

Do all little girls dream of murder?

Sometimes I sneak into their room. When my father's at work, and my mother is... wherever she runs off to, I take my time—lay on their bed, dress in their clothes. But on nights like tonight, I don't have that luxury. It's a quick in, a quick out. The risk of getting caught thrills me.

My mom's underwear drawer had the scent of cedar infused with lavender. I lifted a pair of crotchless panties and held them up to the light.

I felt naughty.

I'd like to put these on and touch myself—lay in bed like an older girl and imagine being used.

I wadded them into a ball and stuffed them in my pocket.

Who'd you like better, your mother or your father? Did you see your parents as a unit, both extensions of themselves, or did one or the other's personality shine? My mother always tried to override my dad.

I was coloring one day—maybe age five or six—using the orange crayon. It reminded me of my him. My mother was brown—dark, but not black—not absolute. I drew an orange man. He looked happy. My mother stepped on him. A light brown wash, and then I pressed darker and harder until, in frustration, the crayon broke. The orange was still there—subdued in some places, overshadowed in others, but still there.

My father always had a way of existing, no matter how hard my mother pressed....

I pulled a black dildo out of her drawer.

For some reason, I held it to my face, inhaled—the strong scent of tea-tree soap. I touched my tongue to it.

Finding a sex toy in your mother's things is weird—especially one this big. I imagined her fucking herself with it—belittling my father. I put the toy back and shut the drawer.

A small dressing table sat by the window. A jewelry box caught my eye. I was about to open it—then I looked out and saw my grandmother standing at the pool house door.

How many life experiences does it take to create insight? My mother was my mother, my father himself, my grandmother always her—Ambrose, I never knew, but I've heard talk. They were all there, and I could see them, not just their personalities—their powers. I always knew what the pieces did, but only recently did I see the dynamic between them.

My mother's comment about the rings was tasteless.

I opened the box and tried on one of her necklaces, the weight of the gold cool against my skin.

I remember when my father gave it to her—Christmas, five years ago. Yeah, had to be five, because I'd just gotten back from boarding school. Anyway, when he held it out to her, she didn't let him put it around her neck. She held out her hand, and when she took possession of it, she tested its weight in her palm—one quick bounce, a scale registering the greed in her heart.

I put the necklace in my pocket.

I'm glad we won't be moving. Maybe my father will fix the pool.

I looked out at my grandmother—the discussion was heated and my father wasn't backing down. He never stood up to her. She was always in—

Fuck! He kicked her—goddamn it. Did you see that? He kicked her.

He let her fall.

Jesus Christ... Why the fuck am I not moving?

My hands were steady. My heart, which had at first jumped, now beat true.

I touched my body like it wasn't mine. I felt nothing. I stood at that window, a TV screen to the years of mother-son conflict, and I didn't scream out. I watched it peak and physically cease. And I didn't care.

My father worked his way into the deep end. He knelt. Praying or speaking to her, I wasn't sure. She wasn't moving.

I needed air. I opened the window.

He looked up at me.

I should have waved.

I pulled out my phone and dialed for the emergency services as my father sat on the steps.

The voice on the other end was as uncaringly human as it gets—one step below robotic. Equal to me.

"911. What is your emergency."

"My grandmother fell."

"Is she conscious?"

"No... I don't think so. My father is with her."

"Are you at— "

"I'm going to hang up now— "

"Wait don't."

I hung up.

I called my mother. "Are you almost home?"

"I'm pulling up now. Why?"

"I think Uma is dead. Dad's with her."

"Are you sure?"

What a thing to ask. Am I sure? Not, what happened, is he okay, are you okay? Just, are you sure.

"Yeah, I'm pretty sure. She fell in the pool."

"I'm coming in."

I made sure her things didn't look disturbed, and then I walked downstairs.

My mother was on the phone as she entered.

"—I'm not sure—hang on." She looked at me. "Did you call anyone?"

"Yeah—I guess they're on their way."

She went back to her call.

"Did you hear her? She said she did, but she can't be sure." My mother checked her reflection in the hallway mirror. "Would you— thanks, Baby."

She slipped her phone into her pocket. "Is your father still out there?"

"Why don't you go check?"

"Rachel, this isn't the time to be a smartass."

"But it's a time to call your boyfriend?"

My mother walked casually into the backyard.

* * * * *

Paula walked by me without a touch. If I hadn't of seen her back, I wouldn't have known it was her.

"Did you check to see if she was still alive?"

I didn't answer.

She took off her heels. Barefoot, she knelt down by my mother's body.

"Don't touch her," I said.

"You didn't even check." Paula picked up her arm, held her hand for a moment, and then stood up. "She's dead."

I caught Paula's eyes as she passed me, her face wearing that just-got-fucked look. I assumed it was Tony—*I'm glad something's satisfying her.*

A moment later a man moved in the opposite direction—fire, rescue.

175

He quickly surveyed the scene and then he gently pulled my mother's body away from the shallow water to check her pulse. I could see where she'd hit her head. She was staring at me with the same look of concern that she always had—blank.

A fireman knelt before me. "Are you her son?"

I looked up him with what felt like a smile on my face, but I guess it didn't read that way.

"Can you tell me your name?"

I felt Rachel's voice, her hand following it to my shoulder. "That's my father, Wesley Wallace. He saw her fall."

A blanket was wrapped around my shoulders.

Jesus, I bet Paula really hates this shit—the attention going to me. I bet she wishes she found her—I bet she wishes she pushed her.

"Did you see what happened?"

"My grandmother fell into the pool. I was looking out the window, and I saw my father try to grab her—but he couldn't."

A stretcher appeared before me. My mother's body was carefully placed on it. As they lifted her arm, her hand hung down, and I noticed one of her rings was missing—the pale white skin called to me.

I stood as her body passed and looked at Paula. She was conversing with a fireman, a feigned look of hurt painted across her face. A four-carat diamond concealed in her pocket.

I rode with my mother's body to County General.

On the way, I asked the paramedic for a plastic bag, then removed the rest of my mother's jewelry. Her wedding ring came off surprisingly easy—the skin tanned beneath. When I was finished, I held the bag out to him.

"Do you hold these things?" I asked.

"Are you afraid of losing them?"

"I was afraid of losing her."

"Why don't we check those in when we arrive—is your wife following?"

"No. I don't want my wife to—I'm sorry, my wife is more scattered than I am. My mother meant the world to her. I'll hold them—it'll be alright."

He placed his hand on my shoulder—a rare moment of human connection.

I've never been a fan of being touched—it hurts more than it soothes—but I let myself feel it, and it wasn't unpleasant.

SPIT ROAST AND HE'S TOAST

The turnout was good. I sometimes forget that the roots of our family are driven deep into this town. It was, however, an aged crowd. If she'd held out longer, half the attendees might have greeted her on the other side.

As you might imagine, the store had been closed for a week. I'm not sure I'm even going to keep it. It had been my way of proving to my mother I was capable—but now, it wasn't necessary.

She was interred in the family crypt—a place I would one day reside, and Rachel too, if she chose. But after her, there'd be no one. I had no male heirs, and I doubt that any man who married Rachel would want his spawn lying in that tomb.

My father—if it's up to me—and now it is, will soon join my mother—*once I learn more about plug-pulling and the like*. I have an appointment with Marcus Blackman tomorrow—the family attorney. We'll go over my inheritance, and my father's imminent burial arrangements.

Dr. Waddell was in his Sunday best—a purple velvet suit.

"No less than your mother deserved, eh, Wesley?"

"Well, if it isn't my favorite shrink. Can't say I'll miss you—that hair-piece of yours is gonna have to find a new beau."

"Oh, I'm sure we'll see each other soon. We've lots to talk about."

"No offense, Terrence, but when you drive off from here, my memory of you is gonna be tied like just-married tin cans to your bumper."

"Oh, Wesley, you really are quite the poet. I can't wait to unpack your mother's passing."

He slid off like a piece of spinach caught on my tooth. I spit, to rid his taste from my mouth.

From my tufted chair in the foyer, I could survey the room, and be available for sympathetic well-wishers.

It was nice of Tony to attend. Fucking my wife or not, it was a touch of kindness on his part. Paula looked as if she was bored.

I guess I should be worried now. What with my mother gone, I'm the only one who stands in the way of Paula living in the comfort of her desire—unless you counted Rachel. But as underhanded as Paula has shown herself, I couldn't see her doing her own daughter in. You never know though. I've heard worse.

"Mr. Wallace?"

I stood to greet him. A distinguished old gentleman clutching a bowler hat in one hand and a cigar in the other—he reminded me of Hitchcock.

"Yes?"

"Tom Burroughs. I was a friend of Ambrose. I wanted to pay my respects."

"It's a pleasure to meet you, Mr. Burroughs. My father spoke highly of you. I'm familiar with your work at the *Sentinel*—you were the voice that all other newspaper men were compared to."

The old man was also known for a recent killing—never charged. You can't judge a man by his stature or his smile. It's only when challenged that the inner beast shows. Burroughs had a reputation for his dogged pursuit of ne'er-do-wells and those who'd commit murder. I hope he's retired.

"I'm sure your father was too kind." He caught my slight flash of

179

distaste and adjusted his take. "A hard man, as we all knew—especially in business, but he had his assets."

"I appreciate you saying so. Thank you."

He put on his hat and shook my hand.

I couldn't help but think he was sizing me up.

He moved off in the direction of Waddell.

"Hey Wes, how's it going?"

It was hard to hate Tony. It wasn't his fault that Paula brought him into this. We all have our dark desires—his just happened to cross mine.

"It's going okay."

"You're handling this better than I could. Hey, I want you to come by for a drink tonight—"

"I don't know, Tony."

"I do. You could use a little relief, and so could I."

"You sure Paula is okay with that?"

"Between you and me, she doesn't have a say... does she?

"No, I guess she doesn't."

The thought of her being held to count by anyone pleased me. The thought of me and Tony lording over her was even better.

A few moments later I saw them arguing in the corner. It wasn't blatant to anyone else, but I knew that look on Paula's face and she wasn't happy.

I walked off to have a coffee.

I felt taller, more of a man... until Paula appeared.

"Tony wants you to come over tonight."

"What about you, Paula? What do you want?"

"I told you."

"No, you told me what Tony wants, not you."

"You want the truth, Wormsie?"

"Are you capable?"

"I think you're asking the wrong question."

"Oh, yeah?"

"You should be asking yourself if you're capable of knowing."

"Paula, if you honestly think that you could still hurt me after everything you've already done…"

"It should've been you, Wesley. I wish you were the one who died. You're a disgusting little man." She brushed imaginary dust from her shoulder. "I had a nice talk with Marcy's parents. I wouldn't count on her coming back to work."

"What are you talking about?"

I looked around the room—Marcy and her parents had been standing near the service bar but they were gone now. What the fuck did she say?

"Ohh, a touch of panic. I guess I *can* still shock you, can't I?" She pulled at my tie, flipped it over my shoulder. "You're so fucking easy, Wormsie. I thought I smelled little-pussy on you. She's our daughter's age for God's sake."

"I'm not sleeping with Marcy."

"I sure hope not. Wouldn't want her getting all tore up on that big cock of yours. Ha!" She purposely adjusted her breasts. "Be there or not, I don't give a fuck."

If it wasn't for Tony, I'd have stayed home.

I was paranoid. If I had a gun, it would've been out and kill ready when I walked up those stairs.

"You're not paranoid, buddy. You're aware."

No shit, huh. If I were Tony—living in this shithole apartment, and I picked up a nice piece of fluff with a comfortable pad, I'd have shot my ass weeks ago. You know Paula's thinking about it. I can hear her now—We thought he was an intruder. He pulled a gun on us. We'd caught him banging his salesgirl, and it set him off.

"I told you to stay away from that fucker—ain't nothing ever right when the fuzz gets involved."

For once, I think you're right, Charles.

I closed the front door but left it unlocked. *If I had to bail, I didn't want to be held up.*

"*What's that fucking smell—oh Jesus, he's fucking her, man.*"

I could hear them in the bedroom—well, I could hear him, and the mumbling pleas of what might have been her. I pushed open the door.

Tony had her tied to the bed—four-point restraints. Pillows had been stuffed beneath her waist to raise her hips, and there was duct tape over her mouth. She looked relieved to see me. Tony was hammered.

The room stunk of booze and sex.

He looked at me and smiled. A bottle of whiskey in his hand—*hold up. A bottle of whiskey* was *in his hand.* He downed it and bounced the empty off the wall. He squinted—one eye closed.

"Take your things off, man. Let's spit-roast this bitch."

I stood there—trying to take it all in, floundering for a way out. "It looks like you got it, Tone—"

"Come on, dude." He put the head of his cock against her ass and slowly pushed it in as she fought to get away. "Pull that fucking tape off her mouth."

I took off my clothes and did as he asked. I wasn't gentle—*yanked not pulled.* She came up screaming.

"Help me!"

"Shut the fuck up, bitch." Tony was in rhythm—sawing back and forth like some Italian fuck machine.

"You're hurting me!"

"Re-tape her, Wes. She ain't ready."

"Please, don't. Wesley, help me!"

Tony shrugged his shoulders. "It's your call, buddy. She's your fucking wife."

He pulled out of her and climbed off the bed. Her breathing heavy as he walked past her into the kitchen.

"Wesley, untie me, please."

"Not, Wormsie?"

I didn't see how freeing her would benefit me. What—untie her, and my cock grows eight inches, she swears her love to me, and I forget about all the times she humiliated me? Nope. She stays put.

Tony returned. "Are you thirsty? I got a cold one."

"No, I'm— "

"Not you, man." He held the bottle to her mouth like he was feeding a baby pig. She swallowed the longneck as he poured—her head pulled back until she vomited on the floor. He slapped her. "You're gonna clean that up, bitch."

I almost felt bad for her.

He looked at me like a judge trying to appease a victim.

"I thought you might like seeing her pay the price. What do you want to do to her?"

"Let her go."

"Really?" His disappointment unmistakable.

"Yeah. This isn't my thing."

I hated her—there was no doubt about that—but, crazy as it sounds, this was too personal. You want to put a pillow over her face and shoot her? Hell yeah, I'm in. But fucking her and torturing her? That's more of a Charles thing.

"Right you are, Wessy. This is my kind of party—she's got an excellent ass, and she can learn to be willing. I get what you're saying, though—about it being too personal. You can always tell when a loved one's pulled the trigger—the face of the deceased is always obscured."

Tony undid the ropes—first her ankles, then her hands.

"I feel like you're judging me, Wes. I'm not, like, all fucked up or something, I just thought we'd try this—she said she was cool with it."

"I did not."

She rubbed her ankles.

Tony tossed a towel over the vomit. The room reeked. We followed her into the living room.

She hadn't bothered getting dressed.

Tony sat naked next to her on the couch. She resisted his kiss at first but then leaned into it. I stood there for a moment, watching, before returning to the bedroom. It was a mess.

I picked up his clothes, folded them, and placed them neatly on the dresser. I laid her things over a chair. I made the bed and turned the covers down. His backup gun and holster were hung over the couch. I went into the kitchen and filled a bowl with warm water and a dash of liquid soap.

"Did you look under the sink?"

Why?

"Come on, Wessy. You're going to handle that piece with bare hands?"

When I passed back through the living room—a pair of yellow kitchen gloves on my hands, Paula was on her knees with his cock in her mouth. Her protests from less than a few moments ago had been forgotten.

I scrubbed the bedroom floor as best I could. The vomit was mostly alcohol. It came up easy. I lit a candle and turned off the lights.

Tony was on top of her when I tapped his shoulder. He rolled off and nodded to me, assuming it was my turn.

"Bring her in here, Tone."

I grabbed her by the hand and led her to the bedroom.

When she laid down on the bed, he still expected me to dig in, but I assured him I just wanted to watch.

For the next forty-seven minutes and fifty-three seconds, I watched as they fucked, drank, fucked again, drank some more, and finally passed out from exhaustion.

Hopefully, they'd stay under until morning.

I got in my car and called Marcy.

"Hello?"

"Hey, Baby. I got the gun."

I picked her up around the corner from her house. She stepped into my car like a bouquet of flowers. I inhaled her as if I was starving for breath—the subtleties of her scent a deluge compared to Tony's foul apartment. I lifted her hair and held it beneath my nose.

"Hey!" she slapped my hand away. "What the hell?"

"It's a long story."

"Where's the gun? Do you have it?"

"Yes, of course."

"It's loaded and everything?"

"It isn't any good if it isn't."

"Can I see it?"

She was like a child—what am I saying, she was acting her age.

"It's in the trunk. I didn't want to get pulled over with that on us."

She relaxed for a moment, shifted into a more mature version of herself, leaned back in her chair, and put her foot on the dash—red tennies, Converse.

"That's a good shoe—you can't trace something like that. I mean, sure, they'll know it's Converse. But no cuts, no unnatural grooves— not a pebble stuck to leave a pattern on a dusty walk. A million fucking people wear that shoe. She's a smart girl—instinct."

"I know." I said it out loud.

She looked at me. "Charles?"

"Yeah."

"What'd he say?"

"He said he likes your shoes."

She let me rest my hand on her thigh as we drove—occasionally squeezing or rubbing—nothing too much.

"Who should I ask?" she said.

"What do you mean?"

"Should I ask you or Charles? What's it like to kill? I want to know everything."

Charles?

"Let me do one, and I'll answer her."

One what?

"Let me do a bum—she doesn't need to do both of 'em."

Who said we were doing two?

"Fuck, Wessy—there's no way you're only doing one. Two's the number. Three if its feeling good and we've got time, but definitely two."

Okay. You want to speak to her?

"Yeah, move over."

He hit the gas—focused, silent, but she knew he was there.

"I got something for you, Charles—a gift."

"Yeah, you got something for me, sis. But I don't want what you're selling."

"Your friend does."

"What friend?"

She reached into her purse, pulled out a large red strap-on, and handed it to him.

"Red?"

"Yeah, I thought it'd fit the mood. What do you think?"

"Ha!" He swung it like a sword, jabbing her in the side before slicing through the air—ignoring the road until a panicked honk snapped him back.

"You're a naughty little girl, sis, but I like you."

"You were going to tell me something."

"Oh yeah—how it feels."

He focused on the road, the dildo resting safely on the dash.

"There are two schools of thought on it. One is anger—you don't want that. It's never satisfied—at least not to my knowledge. The killing alleviates it for a moment, and it feels pretty good, but then it comes back—worse.

The second way, though, that's my favorite. It's a job. I owe my actions to a greater plan. I'm an agent; they're just representatives of wrong. I don't feel much about it other than a sense of accomplishment. I like my job, but I'm not putting in overtime, if you know what I mean."

"Does it change you?"

"Why don't we find out."

He pulled over to the side of the road, got out, and opened the trunk. He took out his new black satchel, slinging it across his chest, then locked the car and put the keys behind the back wheel.

"Why did you do that?"

"I've lost the keys before—a fight, resistance, things get scattered in the scuffle, and you're rushing to get away. Also, what if something happens to me—"

"Could it?"

"I doubt it. Not on this kind of thing, but you never know. If something did, I'd want you to get away."

I came to holding her hand in a parking lot. Charles had slipped back into the shadows. I couldn't remember how I got there—the previous scene cut from my life.

"Where's the car?" I asked.

"It's over there."

She pointed to the other side of the railroad tracks. "You said it was better to walk our way out, instead of running away from the action."

"I did not—oh, I get it. Charles said."

"Do you always disappear when he arrives?"

"I guess so. It just started happening recently. Normally, we'd just talk."

"He said he wanted you to pull your pants down."

"Why?"

"Just do it."

I unbuttoned my pants and lowered my zipper.

"Here." She reached into her bag and pulled out a large rubber cock.

"Red?"

"I thought it fit the mood. Charles liked it."

She pushed my balls through the loop and buttoned my pants around the shaft. I looked like an X-rated Pinocchio.

"Hope this thing isn't reflective. You test it?"

She reached down and gave it a hard yank.

"Owww! Marcy! Fuck, man!"

"Consider it tested. Let's go."

I put the gloves on, unzipped the bag, and pulled out the gun. It felt good in my hand.

"Do you wanna go first, Marce, or let me?"

She thought about it a moment. "I don't know if I'm ready. I want to, but I don't know."

"How 'bout I get the first one, and you can grab one or two as we go?"

"Will it be loud?"

Charles?

"There's a train that rolls through here at 10:45. You got the freeway, the traffic at the port, cars on the highway. This place doesn't know silence. Five shots—do it like this: Hello—pop. Hello—pop, pop. Hello."

"Yeah, it's gonna be loud."

Charles' plan was solid: circle the camp, cut a direct line back, casually killing along the way, and slip into the car.

We held hands as we walked through a field of homeless men bedded down for the evening. She was on my left, the gun in my right.

"Don't go for the head." Charles said, "hit the chest."

NOT A ONE TIME THING

"Let me smell the barrel again."

She couldn't get enough of it.

"I like that. It's like burning metal. Did you think I was gonna do it?"

"I didn't know."

I'd let her kill one. She slipped on the gloves and, with them, slipped off her ability to care.

"He fucking said hello to me. I couldn't believe it. Did you see it? 'How you doing, pops?' Hello—bang. I hit him in the chest, Wesley. Just like you said."

She wiggled in her seat, a childish grin plastered across her face.

I was concerned. Either she was genuinely thrilled by the shooting— troubling enough on its own—or she was trying to convince herself it was okay.

"What does Charles think?"

"He's not around."

She smelled her hand, tapped her foot on the floorboards, and squeezed my leg. "I bet he'd be stoked if he was here. I hope we get to do it again—fuck, I can't go home like this. I'm pumped. Let's do something."

"I've gotta clean this gun and get it back."

"Do you think they know it's gone?"

"Don't say shit like that."

She laughed—a wild, night laugh that pressed against the car's windows. A killer's laugh.

"Do you have a hard time calming down, Boss? I feel like I should go running. Take me to the cop's house with you. I can't go home."

"I think you need to remember why we're doing this."

"What are you talking about? You said I was gonna get a chance to kill somebody, and I did—pop, pop, old man. Did you see the look in his eyes? How many did you do—three, yeah?"

It was three. The first one never even woke up. He might've been dead already. Shooting people is like shooting cows. Dull, unaware, and—depending on the shooter—not afraid.

She wasn't slowing down—tapping a beat on the dash, smacking her gum, giggling as she twirled her hair.

"Do you feel anything, Marcy? Beyond excitement?"

"I feel good. What's wrong with you?"

"It's just a question."

"No, it isn't. You're a real fucking drag, Wesley. If you asked me whether I saw your bullet tear through that boy's hand as he covered his face—that'd be a question. And my answer would be, yes. I loved it. But you're trying to get me to look inside and stir a bunch of shit that doesn't need to be messed with. No. I don't give a fuck about a handful of nameless hobos who spend their days with nothing but basic existence in their heads. They don't add shit, Boss Man. Don't mean a thing to me. Was it fun? Yeah, it was fun. Will I do it again? I don't know. Maybe it was a one-time thing, but I sure hope not. Goddamn it, you fucking faggot.

"You got reasons for doing this shit, but it doesn't mean everyone else has to. Life isn't always connected, guy. It's the curse of the intellectual to think the universe has patterns that we can read. I liked pulling the trigger. I was at home bored when you called.

"No wonder you ended up with Paula. You don't know how to date. You don't know how to let a girl have a good time without asking if it felt good. You can take me home now. I'm done."

Paula's car was still parked where she'd left it. The door was unlocked, and the single light in the kitchen glowed dimly. The apartment was silent.

I walked quietly into the bedroom.

Tony wasn't in bed.

For a moment, panic flared. A week ago, I might've screamed out my guilt. But I was better now—cooler, casual, collected. It was business as usual. I'd shoot him if I had to.

I had the gun in my hand, freshly cleaned in the alley behind the shopping center. He'd never know it'd been fired.

He walked out of the bathroom—still naked, still hard. "What are you doing, Wes? Quit playing with that."

The gloves on my hands went unnoticed. I slid the .38 back in the holster and stepped away.

He was still slurring his words. "I thought you left."

He pulled the covers off Paula, scratched his ass, and held out his cock. "Take your pick, buddy."

I couldn't suck off someone that I was gonna frame for murder. It didn't seem right.

I crawled between Paula's legs and went to work.

It wasn't that bad. Things were looking up.

TRUST FUND BABY

The law offices of Blackman, Devers, and Kroft occupied the 16th floor of the Downtown spire. I hadn't been here since the spring of my eighth year, when my father brought me along for one of his business dealings. The building was beautiful—once hated when first erected, but now it's become a fixture of Ocean Park's skyline.

I took the elevator up, though I planned to take the stairs down— *I've never been a fan of enclosed spaces or loss of control, but walking up sixteen flights was too much.*

The elevator doors opened to reception.

Old money is quiet.

I wish I wore the dark grey suit—the forest green tie was fine, but with this black coat, I feel like a pimp.

I didn't have to wait.

Marcus Blackman the third met me in the foyer. He was ancient, yet impeccable—black suit, red tie, high cheekbones, wavy silver hair over pale blue-grey skin. "Mr. Wallace. It's a pleasure to see you."

"Just Wesley. When I hear Mr. Wallace, I look for my father."

"Ambrose *was* an imposing man."

We moved into his office where he laid out the holdings of the Wallace Family Trust.

It was more extensive than I thought—and to be honest, I hadn't thought much. My parents never discussed finances with me. Why would they? I was, in their words, incorrigible, incompetent, and ill-fitted for responsibility.

I felt a wave of resentment.

We barely covered our bills, and I was often in financial fear. With all this wealth at her disposal, my mother had still forced me to work in that shop and pay her rent.

Blackman caught my thoughts.

"Ambrose wanted you to know what it was to struggle as most do. He didn't want you to be a 'spoiled rotten' trust fund child."

"I'm fifty-two. When the hell were they going to tell me I didn't have to work?"

"I'm afraid you do."

"Excuse me?"

"Under the conditions of the trust, you are to maintain steady employment until the age of fifty-five—although, your monthly endowment is now quiet substantial."

"But I still have to work?"

"Yes. Keeping the shoe store open is strongly encouraged, but the job itself is arbitrary—it's your choice."

"So, I only have three more years to retirement?"

"Yes, that's very amusing, Mr. Wallace."

"I'm gonna get a job at that chicken place—flipping biscuits."

"Are you interested in being a chef—"

"Fuck no—" I caught myself. *It wasn't his fault.* "I apologize for the language. I was making light of the situation. Is there anything else I need to know—stipulations and such?"

"There is. You are to remain under the care of Dr. Waddell at Greenwood, and your father is to remain in state until he succumbs to a natural death."

I didn't know which to attack first. I went with my father.

"Natural? He's been on a goddamn respirator for twenty-four years.

What the hell's natural about that? And Waddell, are you kidding me? He's a money sucking quack! My mother dies, and he's hounding me for a session. There's gotta be a way out of this."

"I'm afraid not. Unless Dr. Waddell retires or expires—"

"Like dead? Expires like dead?"

He gave me a look that I could only describe as complete incomprehension.

"I'm teasing."

"Yes, I do remember your father saying that you were quite the jokester."

We sat in silence for a moment. I wondered if he was still breathing.

"So, other than that, is there anything else I need to know? My Rachel, for instance."

"Other than care at Greenwood, Rachel Ann is under the same conditions as you—to hold employment until the age of fifty-five. And like your father, you are to have a natural death."

"What about her paying rent—all that other crap?"

"Those are not conditions of the trust. As the beneficiary, you're free to spend the monthly allotment as you see fit—as is your daughter— when her time comes. There is no need to be as draconian as your parents."

I shook his hand, a firm cold grip. "Thank you, Mr. Blackman. Is there anything I need to do for you?"

"Short of accepting my apology for that unnecessary quip, we are good to go." He stood and unlocked a leather briefcase at his feet. "Given your current arrangement, I took the initiative to cut you a small check to assist with transition." He handed me a plain white envelope. "I know you've been banking with First Trust, but if you'd like to open a new account downstairs, they could cash that and help you on your way."

I thanked him and took the elevator down.

I had $25,000 in my pocket, and I sure as hell wasn't going to risk *getting robbed in the stairwell.*

"What do you want?"

Paula wasn't always pleasant when I called.

"I just got out of the lawyer's office. I'd like to have a nice family dinner tonight?"

"How'd it go?"

"It went good. We can talk about it tonight."

"Give me a number."

"I don't know. How about five-thirty."

"Not the time, dumbass—how much?"

"How much what?"

"Money. You said it went good. How much?"

"It's not like that, Paula."

"Then what the hell are we having dinner for? I was supposed to go out with Tony."

"Invite him over."

"So, it *did* go good—you're a fucking tease."

"I'll see you at five-thirty."

"Aren't you gonna say it? Come on..."

"Say what?"

"You know—don't make me ask."

"I love you?"

"That's my baby."

She hung up.

I went down to the Green and bought a jade bracelet for Paula, along with a set of tarot cards, some dragon's blood oil, and a witchy book of spells for Rachel. *I don't think she really believes in that crap, but the pictures were cool. She'd like it.* For Tony, I bought a bottle of 20-year bourbon. Close to a grand, but I figured I owed him that much for taking Paula off my hands. Besides, the cash would flow now.

I wished Marcy could come.

I called her.

"Hey, Marcy."

"What's up, Mr. Wallace?"

"I was just thinking of you. I got the trust straightened out today."

"Good for you."

"I wanted to do something nice for you."

"I don't need your money, Wesley."

"I know but—"

"What do you know? You don't know a fucking thing about me."

"Come on."

"Did you want something?"

"Yeah, look if it's about the other night, I'm sorry for what I said."

"Tell me what upset me."

"When I said that—"

"Look, asshole. When you can figure out what you did, let me know. Until then, enjoy the money—fucking tool."

She hung up.

I called back. Straight to voicemail.

Paula had ordered take-out and hung my mother's scarf and cane over one of the empty seats. The table was nicely set—eight bottles of wine for three adults—one of whom didn't drink—our best holiday ware, and the good linen cloth, which carried a faint musty smell. I couldn't remember the last time we used it.

Paula was deep into the vino by the time I arrived—a slight dinner party slur in her words.

I handed out the gifts and poured myself a glass. Tony seemed preoccupied, his eyes constantly darting to his phone. He held up the bottle of bourbon and nodded his approval.

"Jesus, Wes. This is quite a gift." Again, his eyes flicked to the phone. "God damn it. I gotta take this."

He moved with purpose into the kitchen.

Paula held her bracelet to the light. The gold charm, with its single diamond, winked in the glare.

"What is this?"

"It's Jade and gold."

"No, the charm. What is it?"

"I don't know, it just looked pretty."

"Ha! That's the evil eye mom."

Paula turned on me. "Is this your idea of a joke?"

"No—Jesus, Rachel, I didn't know what it was. I thought the color would look good on you—and gold, you like gold."

Tony rejoined the table. "The green matches her eyes." *Paula's eyes were brown.* "I think it's a great gift. Very generous."

Paula took off the bracelet and put it back in the box. "Everything, okay, Tone?"

"Yeah, multiple homicide last night. I got the case."

"I bet you did, fucker."

Charles not now.

I wiped my mouth. "Do you say congratulations for something like that?"

"I'd like to congratulate the guy who did it."

"He's sitting right here, bitch. You're welcome."

"What happened?"

"Well, as far as we can tell, it was random—you know how hard it is to get a story out of those guys—half of them are sauced out of their minds, and the other half either don't speak English or they're just fucking retarded."

"What guys?"

"The homeless. I guess a couple walked through that camp over by the Stockyards and they wasted four random victims—a boy, fifteen, and three older men—no connection whatsoever."

"A couple—a couple of what?"

"No, Wes. A couple, like a man and woman—it doesn't make any sense."

Rachel held up one of the bottles of wine and read the label. "No wonder Uma moved to the desert."

"Can you stop calling her that now?" I looked at my mother's saved seat as if she were sitting there—*that scarf must be forty years old. I think she once threatened to choke me with it.*

"I'd like to stop talking about death at the table." Paula raised her glass. "To life!"

We joined her.

She looked at me like I was dessert. "So, what's the big news, dear? Are you swimming in green?"

"Ha! Finally, that cunt says something amusing."

What the fuck are you talking about?

"Your mother—swimming in green—ha! That's a kick."

Fucking Charles— leave me alone.

"No. Not really."

"No?"

"It's a trust Paula. I receive a monthly stipend under certain obligations."

Tony chimed in with a pretty cool pirate voice. "There be rules, 'ey Wesley?"

He really wasn't that bad—likeable, and like me, more than Paula deserved.

"That's right, Tony—one being that I need to be gainfully employed for another three years."

Paula couldn't give a fuck. "What about me?"

It was always about her.

"Nothing changes for you, dear. You're not listed."

"That's ridiculous. Everything stays the same? Then what the hell are you bringing us these gifts for?" She tossed the boxed necklace into the center of the table. "Fuck you."

"Mom!"

"Oh, fuck that, Rachel." She pointed at the empty chair with her glass. "We lived under that old woman's thumb and now we're living under this."

She stood up, glaring at me. "I bet you love this shit, don't you? Your little ways of keeping us under your will."

"Paula," I glanced at Tony, who was back on his phone. "I have no desire to control—"

"Oh God, here comes another one of his blah, blah, blah talks about whatever the fuck he's gonna go on about. What's it this time, Wormsie?"

Tony stood—unconcerned with Paula's foul behavior. "I gotta go." He grabbed his bourbon, kissed Paula's cheek and patted my mother's chair. "Thanks, Wes."

"What a fucking joke." Paula downed her glass.

"Sweetheart, if you'd let me finish."

"Go ahead." She poured herself heavy. "This wine will outlast your rant."

"What I was going to say is: I now receive a substantial monthly living allowance—much more than I expected. You and Rachel—other than the ability to afford a much higher standard of living—are not affected under the rules."

"Why the fuck didn't you just say that? More of your bullshit games." She held up her glass. "Congratulations, Rachel—your father's an asshole."

She grabbed an unopened bottle and made her way upstairs.

Rachel cleared the table. "Have you ever thought of divorcing mom?"

"No. I don't believe in it—neither does she."

"So you believe in being bullied and cheated on?"

"It's not cheating if you know about it—I'm grateful for Tony. He gives her something I couldn't."

She picked up the plates. "You know, you wouldn't even have to divorce her."

"Yeah, maybe she'll get fed up and walk away—$50,000 a month won't keep her around."

"Shit, Dad! Are you kidding me? 50k?"

"That's the number."

"Well, don't tell mom that. You'll never lose her… unless."

"Unless what?"

"I could always whip you up a little cocktail—a protein drink with a dark kick."

"Rachel! Don't ever!"

"Jesus, Dad. I was only kidding." She sniffed an open bottle of wine and poured the last few drops into her mouth. "Lighten up."

When Rachel went to her room, I took my glass and stepped out into the yard. I needed air.

Upstairs light shadowed the shallow end of the pool, but the deep end glowed—gave the brackish water an almost inviting aura.

I learned to swim in this pool. My dad taught me—the John Wayne method: toss me in and retrieve my body if I drowned. But at least he held me for a moment before he threw me in. I did all right and I paid him back later—albeit unintentionally.

Beyond the pool—two acres of what used to be showpiece garden paths. I walked out as far as the small bridge—ornamental, Japanese style, painted red. There was a small spring here.

I bet if we cleaned this up, I could move that pool house to the far end—or shit, why move it? I'll just have it recreated.

I looked back toward the house. The window. Rachel, looking out over the deep end. My mother, reaching for help.

I wonder if she saw me pull my hand away.

That quip about poisoning Paula? Too casual to be a joke.

Daddy's girl, huh? Maybe.

YOU AGAIN?

"So, we meet again, Wesley."

I had no idea bad breath could fill a room so completely. It was as if a feta gas leak had sprung beneath the sofa.

"Look, Terrence."

"Dr. Waddell."

"Fuck that. My mother's dead. I can call you anything I want—you're lucky I don't beat your ass."

"Oh, Wesley. I guess we need to establish our parameters, don't we?"

Another wave of sour air—pickled onions and tahini dressing. I'll never eat Greek again.

"You are to see me twice a month, and I am to submit my recommendations to Blackman and associates."

"What about client privilege and all that nonsense?"

"Can I discuss what you say? Of course not. Can I suggest you be recommitted as a danger to yourself or others? You bet your little boots I can."

He spun a pencil in his hand and dropped it awkwardly. It rolled across the desk and onto the floor.

"If I remember right"—he glanced at his notepad—"you threatened to 'beat my ass' when you arrived."

"Come on, Waddell—Dr. Waddell. That's just something guys say."

"That's a fucking joke—could you imagine this motherfucker beating on anyone—yeah, beating on their dicks."

I laughed.

"Is that amusing, Wesley?"

"No, of course not. I apologize. You know I'm not a violent man."

Waddell lowered his glasses, peering over the frames at me.

"I guess I'm just upset about my mother."

"Let's speak on that."

"I'd rather not."

"Too soon? I found it interesting that your mother and your father both had accidents in the backyard of that home—albeit your mother's was a touch more serious."

"My father has been as good as dead for the last twenty-four years—I consider that pretty serious."

"But not dead, yes?"

"No. Not dead."

"Excellent—not his state, of course, but your acceptance of it. And how is that 'acceptance of self' going?"

"You know what I think, Wessy? I say we waste this motherfucker—rape, torture, kill—not necessarily in that order."

"What?"

"I said your acceptance of self, Wesley."

"I wasn't talking to you."

"Ha, now you did it."

"Excuse me?"

"I spoke out loud—went over something in my head and said it by mistake."

"Let's flip through their directory of shrinks. If we find a nice little Asian broad with thick lips and a fat ass—we whack this fucker and trade up."

Goddamn it, Charles—shut up.

"Pop, Pop, Pop, little piggy."

"Wesley?"

"Yeah?"

"Are you hearing voices again? Outside agitators stirring things up?"

"No, of course not."

"Wesley?"

"Look, Doc, it's like you said. Acceptance is a process. I'm better at it than I was before, but there's room for improvement."

"That there is."

I was hit by another blast of foul air—the scent this time unrecognizable.

"I apologize for how I came in. I know seeing you is good for me."

"Don't just play me, Wesley. I can see through a ruse."

"Can you see through a set of black eyes, bitch?"

"I'm not playing you. My daughter deserves a healthy father."

"Ah, Miss Rachel." He checked his watch, jotted her name on his pad. "Hopefully, we can visit with her next session."

There was another "ticket" on my windshield. I filed it in the glovebox under a used pair of Marcy's panties.

I'd forgot they were there.

I held them to my face. She smelled good—the scent of her body and perfume still clinging to the cloth.

A knock at my window. A large shadow loomed.

His thick tongue forced out the words. "You... you can't park here—only doctors."

I turned toward his voice, her panties still covering my nose and mouth. "Mphhh?"

"You can't park here."

He was one of Greenwood's "special officers." His hat comically cocked on his head, his shirt untucked.

"Look at that little guy—he's sure doing his thing, huh?"

What's with you and these people? He's a retard, Charles.

"He's an innocent, for fuck's sake. Compare this little man to that asshole Waddell or that bitch wife of yours. He ain't got a mean bone in his body. Look at him—an innocent."

I took the panties off my face and rolled down my window. Charles was right. There was no reflection of evil in his eyes, no hidden score waiting to be settled. I read his badge.

"I'm sorry, officer Mike. I should have known better."

"You should." He looked down at his ticket book, his pudgy hands nervously squeezing the imitation black leather.

I didn't have the affinity that Charles did, but a good deed done might help me—karma and all that.

"Thank you for doing a good job, officer. I'll let the gate know you're on it."

He stood as tall as his large, hunched frame would allow—all five foot eight, two hundred and two pounds of him.

"I'm… I'm Officer Mike Mays—that's me."

"I'll let 'em know."

I pulled out of the parking lot and stopped near the front gate. I had her in my nose. I had to try.

I called her. Voicemail—"…phone number and leave a message please."

"Marcy." I took a shot. "I apologize for trying to analyze you and connect you to my plans. I realize that you are your own person and that your reasons are your own."

The line clicked. Then her voice—"Continue."

"From now on, I'll make it my duty to take your considerations seriously, and I accept—and welcome—any corrections you might suggest."

She hung up.

I waited a few moments and sent a text:

I'm going over to the shop. Air it out. Check the mail. If you're not busy, I'll be there until four.

As I passed through Greenwood's gates, her reply popped:

With Pay?

Yes, with pay.

At the shop, there were a few bouquets of flowers and a candle placed at the front door. The candle had burned down to nothing—just empty glass. But the saint on the label had survived. Saint Homobonus.

"What the fuck? Somebody's fucking with you, Wessy. Ain't no saint named that—the nerve of 'em—your mother lying dead. Pray for us, oh, Holy Boner."

Knock it off asshole.

I glanced over my shoulder at Rocco's. A drink wouldn't hurt. I set the candle down, the saints face turned inward.

"That's it, Wessy. Get liquored up and beat somebody's ass!"

The place was empty but for the bartender—a ginger, bright red hair, freckles.

"How you doing?"

"I own the shop across the street."

"I know. I've seen you. I heard you were in the other night. Did your buddy make it home alive?"

"Yeah, thank you. I drove."

"Me too—a couple of cocktails, and I'm behind the wheel." He wiped the bar with a pair of boxers. "I read about your mother. Sounded like quite a woman. What can I get you?"

I checked my watch. "It's still pretty early. How about a salty dog?"

"Yes—a solid morning beverage."

He set my drink on the bar.

"How much?"

"Come on, buddy," he poured himself a shot. "For your mother." He held his glass up—a toast.

"Thank you."

We saluted, and I took a drink. The cool, grapefruit juice against the vodka was perfect—the salted rim, sublime.

"You didn't happen to see who left the flowers did you?"

"We left the wreath…"

"And the candle? St. homo—was that a joke?"

"I take my saints seriously." He reached behind him and pulled another St Homo from his shelf, setting it down and lighting it. "The patron saint of merchants and Charity workers. The *Sentinel* said your mother was a patron of Greenwood. My father was there." He took another shot. "In memoriam eius!"

"Latin?"

"Yeah—bout the only thing I ever learned."

"I'm not a big God guy."

"Then you need a bigger God."

He had a sobriety coin on a chain around his neck.

"Thank you for the drink… and the saint lesson. You learn something new every day."

He poured himself another shot and tossed it back. "You do if you're open—you gotta stay open."

I guess "sobriety" is self-defined.

The air inside the store was thick with the scent of neglect.

It's odd how quickly something can sour when you let it go. When I first met Paula, the taste of her skin was like water in the desert. Not anymore. Now she tasted of old milk—weight, burden—stagnant and foul.

The stereo sat in the corner, small speakers wired through the shop. I put on a jazz channel—piano pieces, bright stars of sound—and let it fill the room.

I left the front door locked, the sign flipped to *Closed.* I wasn't in the mood to entertain customers, but I turned the lights on as if we were open.

At my desk, I powered on my computer and opened his file.

Charles' world lit up my screen, painted in text. I ran my finger across the words. I like playing God, though free will truly exists under my hands.

"Make it sweet, buddy—real nice."

I don't control you, Charles. You just do what you do.

DEBBIE DOWNER

We walked to the park, hand in hand. I'd love to say it was perfect—it was set up that way, but with each breath she damned me. Her weight of innocence couldn't mask my guilt. Her kindness exposed me.

"I want to watch the boys, Charles. The boats."

"I thought you wanted to feed the geese."

"The ducks bite."

"Do you blame them?"

She stared at me, confused. She had no idea what I was saying.

"They think you're candy." I kissed her neck.

A woman pushing a stroller did a double-take as she passed.

"I forgot the bread, Charles." She slapped her head in frustration. "I'm a dummy."

I held her close.

"You're perfect, my love. I like the boats. Those geese are assholes."

It's easy to forget who you are when the world you exist in is yours. I pulled my hand away from hers and wiped the sweat on my pant leg.

The lake stretched wide, a vast expanse of grey blue water. I sat on a bench, watching as she approached the boys. I felt protective.

"Charles, come here."

A young boy was letting her hold his boat—a three masted schooner.

He hovered nervously, worried she might drop it. I reached them just as the boy's father took the vessel from Debbie's hands.

"She wasn't going to drop it," I said.

Debbie walked off, unaffected.

"I'm sorry, sir. It's an expensive toy."

"How much is she worth?"

"Excuse me?"

I nodded toward Debbie. "How much is she worth?"

"I meant no offense."

"But you did offend me. How much for the boat?"

"It's not for sale."

"Neither was she. How much for the boat?"

"Charles!" Debbie called, oblivious. An old man was reeling in a fish. "Charles!"

I couldn't stop myself. As I've told you before, it's not anger. No build-up, no escalation. I'm one way, then another.

I grabbed his boy by the arm and yanked it out of the socket. Screams tore through the air. The father came at me hard. Sadly, stock investing and weekend golf outings do not a pugilist make. I punched him in the throat as he approached, then stomped on his neck when he fell. The boy, arm hanging limp at his side, I surrendered to the muddy waters of the lake. The schooner, I dispatched with my heel.

One way, then another—an agent writing wrongs.

It seemed as if the whole park was running toward me, and I, like a rabid dog off-leash, ran towards them, snarling and spitting. I passed a stunned Debbie, standing, smiling, a blank stare on her face.

I left her at the mercy of the mob.

I ran across Fifth and up the alley behind the theatre. When I reached the old armory. I called for him.

Wesley!

"I'm here."

Is she okay?

"They don't think you knew her. The police are looking for you."

Is she okay?

"What did you expect? She's scared, heartbroken, doesn't know why you left."

What about the boy?

"He'll be okay—Jesus, you couldn't just walk away?"

I couldn't. It's like it rooted me to the spot, then worked its way up from my stomach. I didn't want to hurt him.

"You pulled his arm out of the socket."

I hurt his father. That prick might've sold the boat, but not his son.

"I don't know what to say, Charles. What are you looking for?"

If I said peace, would you laugh?

"Of course not."

Do you think you'll always hate your mother, Wesley?

"Where the fuck is that coming from? I don't anymore. She's dead."

So, you're over doing the things you did while she was alive—her influence?

"Where are you going with this?"

I need this off me. Thought being with Debbie would help, but it made it worse. I want to get rid of this hate—this fucking guilt.

(Sirens, a block away, toward the park.)

Should I go back? I bet she's scared.

"I wouldn't."

Marcy dropped her shop keys on my desk. I looked up at her, smiled, and then I wrote my last line.

Click, click, click—punch.

That night, I slept in the bushes across the street from her place. Mary's car was there until the morning. I thought about knocking on the door, throwing myself at Debbie's feet, but I figured it was better to let her hurt now than to keep hurting her.

I'm a piece of shit.

I saved the file and clicked out.

"Charles?" she said.

"Yeah."

"How's he doing?"

"He's in the bushes outside Debbie's house."

"Debbie?"

"His girlfriend, Debbie. She has Down syndrome, and he just ripped some boy's arm out of the socket."

She looked at me like I didn't matter.

"Where do you get this shit?"

"I don't know. I don't make it up. It just sort of appears."

"Can we talk to Charles?"

"I think he's gone. I don't feel him."

"And where are you, Boss Man? Are you here?"

"Yes." I got down on my knees, held her ankles, and touched my forehead to her shoes. "I'm here—for now."

IN THE LINE OF DUTY

"Am I on the clock?" She took out a cigarette, gave it a lucky tap, and then fired it up.

I was about to protest, but why bother.

"I was thinking back to when I first walked into this shop. Was that Wesley—this Wesley—or have you changed?"

"I'm not sure what you're talking about."

"Where does the act start, Boss Man, and the real you end?"

She grabbed a coat from the rack—leopard print, trashy.

"Do you honestly think anyone is real? Look at you, Marcy—walking in here with your baggage in tow. Did you rehearse the part you were going to play?"

"I like older men, Chief. I smelled something on you that appealed to me." She twirled in front of the mirror. "You saw me as something to use—your little jerk-off fantasy stepping in here like a bad porn movie."

She deepened her voice—sultry, slutty.

"Do you need a salesgirl, sir?"

I laughed when she said it.

"So, you smelled something on me, I used you, but somehow I'm the actor?"

She ashed on the rug, and lowered her eyes—laid the power in my hands before snatching it away with a laugh.

"You're so fucking easy, Wesley."

She sounded like Paula. I wasn't sure whether to feel humiliated or proud.

"Do you think you're capable of being honest, Boss Man?"

"I don't know."

She laughed. *This was fun for her, this cat-and-rat game she was playing.*

"That's the first truth we've ever shared."

"What about the uh…"

"Don't bother. I know what you are, Wesley. What I want to know is what you're planning. And don't forget—although it seems so long ago—I still have the files. If something happens to me, you're fucked. So, tell me—what's on your mind? Is it worth sticking around for?"

When I got home, Tony was sitting in the living room. He wasn't drunk, but he wasn't sober either. He'd been suspended.

When you're small, and not angry, and have nothing to prove, you are wary when dealing with the erratic emotions of a large, violent man.

I had to step lightly. The story was his to tell. I could do my best to coax it from his mouth, but I couldn't pull.

"Fucking crybaby cocksuckers. I hate these motherfuckers. No wonder the city is falling apart."

He poured heavy.

I held out my glass. "Can I join you?"

"Join me?" He poured deeper than I'd normally go. "You don't want to join me, Wes. Fucking suspended, man. Can you believe that? I'm twice decorated, and that fucking wig-wearing cunt pulls my ticket."

"They shouldn't let women run the force."

"Ha! That's fucking funny, bud. He ain't a bitch—he's a wig-wearing queer. I was right. This town's a fucking mess. And when an officer of the law can't let off a little steam when the shit gets high, what can we do?"

"What'd you do, Tone?"

"I said, "Nice shot.""

"What?"

"It was a nice shot. That fucking shooter put one right between that old fuck's eyes—I mean, you could have literally put a measurement on either side, and it was dead on."

I remember that one. I even said hello first. I was supposed to stick to the body, but when I brought the gun up, there was something about his head that just said, hit me.

"That's ridiculous, T."

"You know how many times I said shit like that—to the fucking chief, man, and he just laughed? And now this woke-ass motherfucker pulls me off the case."

There was a copy of the Sentinel on the table. He'd made the front page—corruption and alcoholism in the line of duty.

Tony spit on the headline.

"I lost my fucking wife and kids—my dedication to this job tore them up. And this is how they repay me, huh—hero to fucking zero. I guess you know what it feels like, huh? Another guy fucking your wife. But I ain't into it—I ain't no bitch."

"Can I get you something, Tony? Something to eat?"

"No—I'm waiting on Paula. Hey, you wanna stop by tonight?"

"Are you up for something like that?"

"I'm always up, motherfucker." He stood, put his boot on the coffee table, and grabbed his cock.

"Ha! Jesus! I was just kidding, Tone—trying to be the man in the wig."

He quick-drew his service piece, pointed it right at me. "You better watch that shit, motherfucker."

"Tony!" Paula burst into the room. "Stop it!"

The big man put the gun back and took another pull. I was surprised that Paula was so protective.

She walked over and put her arm around his waist. "My baby's had a tough day, Wesley." She kissed his neck. "He's doing bath and bed tonight."

"Yeah...not." He took a big drink. "I'm doing pussy and ass tonight, bitch. And maybe, if I'm feeling up to it, I might shoot me a couple bums. Ha!"

He punched my shoulder as Paula steered him towards the door. "See ya later, buddy."

Paula sighed. "Tonight?"

"Every night, bitch. Every fucking night."

I watched out the window as she loaded him in the car—*I should say, her new car—my new car. It's my fucking car—bought with my money.*

I pulled out my phone. The picture was shit—nothing but pocket, but the audio was clean:

"I'm doing pussy and ass tonight, bitch. And maybe, if I'm feeling up to it, I might shoot me a couple bums. Ha!"

I couldn't have asked for better.

I took a hot shower and washed my hair.

I don't like the way the water feels on my skin. I remember telling Old Doc Hobbs at Greenwood that it hurt to be touched, and that the shower amplified that. Those were different days. They used to force me to shower—exposure therapy, they called it. I called it pain, humiliation, a lesson in distrust. If you hurt someone long enough, and hard enough, they will strike back.

The razor was sharp. My moves, precise.

"Put some of that frou-frou on—the one I like."

"The Bay Rum?"

"Yeah, you ever try to drink it, Wessy?"

"Nah, not that."

215

"But the mouthwash, yeah?"

"Yeah, sometimes."

"And the pills?"

"Yeah, Charles. Always the pills."

"It's good being bigger now, huh?"

"Do you think you're funny?"

"Ah, come on, man. I ain't talking about size. I'm talking about age. You can do what you want now—and you got a little green to make it easier."

"You think money helps?"

"I don't know—maybe."

"Would it have helped with Debbie?"

"I'm gonna take care of her."

"What do you mean by that?"

Silence.

"Charles… Charles… Hello?"

They call it 'lying in wait' but that's not what I'm doing. I'm not waiting. The moment is done, visualized, completed—and I will set her free.

I once heard Wesley talk about lying. Now normally, I think he's out of his fucking mind—and that does benefit me, as you do know—but the other day, he thought about something legit. He'd been reading this quote, some bullshit about truth setting you free, and my man, Wessy said no, the truth is not freedom. The truth grounds you in the present. It's a chain that holds us back. It's the lie that frees us, inflames us—the lie is imagination, seeing ourselves as better than we are.

I tried to lie with Debbie, believing that her purity could heal me, but she was incapable of lying. And so, I fell. If she could've stepped away from reality, I could see us with real lives—and maybe children or something. I don't know if she's capable of that. But maybe, maybe we could've.

I watched Mary pull up. She had on one of those shirts with a cute little picture—puppy, maybe a bear. Clueless.

I think what someone dies in is important. I could give you two or three incidences where the right outfit would've got more play. It's like pajamas—if you're gonna shoot a kid, do it when he's in his pajamas. Hell of a picture.

I followed her up the stairs.

There wasn't a lot of life in Debbie's building. Short of a fire or a goddamn sonic boom, I couldn't see anyone coming to check things out.

"Fuck... Hey, Siri?"

"Uh-huh."

"Can you do me a favor and send a message to the Matador?"

"What would you like me to say?"

"Don't forget to call somebody about Debbie. I love you, Charles."

Yeah, I call myself the Matador—no reason, really, I just like it. Never had a friend to give me a nickname. Always wanted one. And the I love you, nobody had ever said that to me either, until Debbie. I think I need that—the reassurance that I ain't all bad.

I brought my .45.

I know some of you are gun nuts, and you'd love this fucker. I got it off an old drunk that was gonna kill himself if he didn't give it away. I was the recipient. It's a beauty. Government-issue M1911.

There was no reason to wear a mask.

I kicked open the door.

I knew Debbie's place. She was a big fan of the 60-watt bulb; the barrel flash from my .45 would be impressive.

I shot Mary in the throat.

As her head snapped back, I put three more in her chest.

I fucked up her shirt a little, but you could still see the dog's legs below the holes, so if you had a good crime writer, he could really dig it.

Debbie was screaming—you can't really hear in those situations.

It's more a thick, continuous hum than single sounds, but I saw her mouth moving, and it wasn't blowing sweet kisses—although she did look beautiful. I pushed her to the floor and put a pillow over her head. I wasn't lying when I told Wessy about that loved one thing.

She was strong—built compact. No match for me, but she fought harder than I expected.

Debbie was perfect, and she was innocent, and without me to look after her, she would continue to be hurt—like those boys in the market, the father by the lake, or another man like me who could see the beauty in her and want to exploit it. I have the power to keep her innocent and unharmed forever.

She stopped kicking and gently grabbed my arm—there was no distortion in the image of her hand. It was pure and clear, and her nails had been recently painted a shade of strawberry blush. She'd done them for me.

I started to cry.

I wasn't an agent. I wasn't doing this world no favors. I was useless. This ain't right.

She squeezed my arm.

I couldn't do it. I couldn't remove the only person who ever really cared for me.

I took the pillow from her face and placed the barrel in my mouth.

NICE SHOT

"Geez, Dad. Look at you all dressed up. Where you going?"

"I'm gonna go hang out with Tony and your mother."

"Really?"

"Yeah, why not."

"Besides the obvious of him being a drunk, and my mother being a bitch."

"Don't say that about your mom, sweetheart."

"Dad, you're hanging out with your wife, and her boyfriend."

"It's complicated."

"I'll say."

She was wearing a t-shirt with no bra and a short skirt riding high on her thighs. I didn't approve, but we'd been getting along so good, I didn't want to rock the boat.

"Where are you going?"

"I'm going out."

"With who?"

"Tyson."

"I thought you were done with him. I don't like him—what are you doing?"

"I guess it runs in the family, Dad."

She put on her sweater, and I noticed the hickeys on her neck.

"Guess we both have a taste for abuse."

Wesley was out of his mind. He was the one preaching discretion when I suggested doing Bradberry, and now he's going to kill his wife and blame it on some cop. It's crazy. And as much as I'd love to get back on the trigger, I don't fancy jail.

"It's a sure-fire plan, Marce. I wait until they're drunk and then I shoot her with his backup gun, and put it in his hand."

"And what then, Wesley? He wakes up and says, 'I did it.'"

"No, I'm gonna shoot her, plant the gun, and let the cops wake him up."

I didn't bother arguing. Guys like Wesley can't listen. They get a plan in their head and right or wrong, it seems they gotta play it out.

"Marcy!"

"Yeah, Mom."

"Your father's ready for dinner."

"Okay, I'll be right there."

I knew what I wanted to do, but I wasn't sure how it was gonna go down. I was hoping Marcy would've helped out but no go. Probably for the best anyway. She was unstable. I didn't need a teenage spree killer in on this one—no matter how good she tasted.

I had my gloves in my pocket. I hoped I wouldn't have to wait all night.

The light was out over his stairs. It was as if he knew what was coming. The front door was open. And there he was.

Charles was waiting for me in the living room.

What are you doing here?

"I tried to kill Debbie."

He was a shadow of himself—full color, holographic, from somewhere beyond reality. He hovered—a specter of past misdeeds over cheap green shag.

Why do you look like that? Why aren't you in my head?

"*I don't know. Why the fuck do you always think there's an answer for everything? I'm here, accept it on face value. I thought about what you were going to do and I wanted to stop you.*"

Why?

"*Do you remember when you loved her?*"

Yeah, of course.

"*You're lying, don't fucking placate me man. Think about it—give me one fucking moment when you loved her, just one.*"

I was struggling to come up with it.

"*You used her from day one.*"

"*She used me.*"

"*No. You took advantage of her. Nobody wanted you. She was drunk. You did it.*"

She forced me to have a child.

"*No, you played against her morals, you manipulated her.*"

She stripped me bare.

"*You flaunted a trophy wife, little man.*"

She cheated.

"*You encouraged it. Did you ever love her? Answer me.*"

I searched my heart and could find no instance of that emotion being tied to her.

"*And now what? You're gonna kill her, and blame it on Tony?*"

Who gives a fuck?

"*There it is—who gives a fuck, not you. And now you're bringing your daughter into this—you're a hell of an actor Wesley—a sparrow with a broken wing, flopping about in a field, drawing wolves to his plight—*"

"*That's right, I'm injured. I'm hurt. I'm small.*"

"*You're a vicious animal, but you don't have to be, you can let this go.*"

I heard them in the bedroom—Tony's heavy thrusts, Paula's moans.

"Why don't you just walk out, go turn yourself in."

You're out of your fucking mind.

"No, I'm not. Watch me." He paused. "I know remorse. I'll show you."

He shimmered into the reflection of the streetlights on the wall.

I took off my jacket and kicked off my shoes.

It was quiet in the bedroom, a brief respite before he pounded her again.

The light was behind me as I stood in the door.

When I stepped in, I was hit in the chest—a great burning pain enveloped me.

Tony's voice. "Paula! What the fuck are you doing? Give me that fucking gun!"

I was still breathing. My right side burned—each ragged breath feeding the flame.

She stood over me, pointed his gun at my chest.

"Paula! Right fucking now! Drop it!"

It's strange what you notice when you're down. She was naked. I could see the marks from her bra around her breasts. Her hair was a mess—hanging down over her eyes, the way hair looks after sex. She wasn't holding the .38, that was my choice. She went for the real thing. Tony's police issue Sig.

"Paula!" His voice again—pleading.

A drop of her sweat stung my cheek, then bled into my mouth—bitter, salty, warm. She wasn't angry—intent, that's the word for her expression. She was cool, calm, collected. I'm not going to say I deserve this, but I do have it coming.

"Paula! Drop it!"

The last pop echoed, spinning her body away from me and dropping her to the floor. I would've told Tony it was a nice shot, but I passed out.

THE RECKONING

Tony was right about the wig. Commissioner Crabtree's hairpiece looked homeless.

"Mr. Wallace, there really is no need for an attorney present. These are pretty standard questions—more fact-finding actually."

I'd been in this hospital bed for just shy of a week. As chest wounds go, I was lucky. Paula was as good at manslaughter as she was at fidelity.

"I appreciate that. But Mr. Grace is here at my request."

"I can assure you, on your end, this isn't a criminal matter. Do you have information about the case?"

"Mr. Grace?"

Blackman, Devers, and Kroft didn't handle criminal cases, but they knew the guys who did. I made a phone call. Mr. Grace arrived.

"My client is willing to provide information to assist your investigation, but he will not testify or make any statements under oath. We can discuss terms under which this information can be shared, ensuring my client's rights and privileges are fully protected."

"Mr. Wallace, this is not a formal investigation. You called me."

Grace was no-nonsense. If he ever smiled, there was no evidence of it on his face.

"Do you agree, Mr. Crabtree?"

"Yes, of course. What is it?"

Mr. Grace nodded to me, signaling his approval, and then stepped to the side, ready to interject if needed.

"Tony saved my life. Paula was going to kill me."

"We're aware of that."

"It's funny though—and I feel terrible telling you this, especially after what he did for me—but I went there to protect her."

"What do you mean?"

"Tony killed those homeless men in that camp. He's a murderer."

"What?"

"Go ahead, you can check it. He used his backup piece—that's what he called it. I have the tape."

Mr. Grace played him the clip—the audio was perfect:

"I'm doing pussy and ass tonight, motherfucker, and maybe, if I'm feeling up to it, I might shoot me a couple bums. Ha!"

The commissioner covered his mouth with his hand, staring through me at the scene forming in his mind—one of his top officers guilty of murder.

"Nice shot," he muttered under his breath. "Goddamn it."

"I won't testify. If that's what you want, I can't do it. He saved my life. But I couldn't stand it if another innocent died. He needs to be off the street."

Crabtree's mind returned to the room.

"But, Mr. Wallace, you must see how we need your testimony to convict."

"No, you don't. My wife—in what I consider one of her last selfless acts—was killed, and, tell me if I'm wrong, with Tony's backup gun. The .38."

"She was."

"Run ballistics—what do they call it? Yeah, forensics. The bullet will match those poor souls he murdered in that field. You don't need me. You know what he is."

At 4:49 p.m., Detective Anthony Acala was driven to the back door of the Ocean Park Central Station, walked through a phalanx of reports, and booked for the murders of Paula Louise Wallace, Benjamin Davis, William P. Richardson. Guillermo, and Angel Sanchez.

At 4:52 p.m., a lone man slipped through the front doors of Ocean Park Central, past a swarm of reporters who paid him no mind. He asked for a detective. He was told to sit on the bench and wait.

"You sure you want to do this, Charles?"

It's not about want, or don't want. I'm just doing it.

"Did you kill Debbie?"

You know I didn't.

"Then why are you doing this?"

Because you won't. You've never been able to see it, Wes—the good in this world. That fucking trickle of love that flows beneath and interconnects everything."

"Are you fucking with me? You don't believe that bullshit."

Yeah, I'm fucking with you—I've never stayed remorseful for long. I gotta do this, though. If there is a God, or some sort of Higher Power, I'm sure He'd want me to confess my crimes and make restitution for my evil ways. I'll see you around.

DADDY DEAREST

I don't know if you've ever been shot in the chest, but it's not an easy heal. They convicted Tony, and I was still hurting. If not for Paula, I'd be worried that he'd dodge the bullet, come after me in reprisal, and make me pay, but he killed his alibi. Ha! I won't say I'm not lonely, though. I got Rachel, sure, and she's been real good to me, but Marcy still isn't taking my calls, and Paula's dead. A man needs companionship. Sometimes I think Charles did that for me—supported me in that way. But I couldn't lay down with him at night. Even Paula, as cold as she was, I could still feel her heat under the covers.

I left Rachel in charge of the house and yard. She did a great job. The pool was back in service, and my office had been torn down and rebuilt in the back.

I was thinking about getting a job, but why would I want a boss when I had my own little porn-generating shop? I could replace the cameras, hire a young assistant, and groom her into the best employee I'd ever had.

I picked up my phone and opened the photo of me, posing on the showroom floor with my first real cock—the royal blue banger. It was impressive. I was the man.

I put on a sweater and walked downstairs—*maybe I could join a club, find a normal girl. Older, more interested in cuddling than cumming.*

"Hey Dad. Got a minute?"

"I got hours. What's up?"

"I made you a shake."

"You never stop with that stuff, do you?"

"Stop? I have a garden out back. I was thinking of maybe starting a business—you know how good I am with plants, maybe rare spices or witchy concoctions."

The shake was delicious. I downed it and wished there was more.

"Uma told me that you used to have a garden."

The memory was uncomfortable—something you think you've buried, but only for it to claw its way back.

"Yeah, I had a little patch in the back."

"She said it wasn't your fault what happened to your father. You didn't know."

She was watching me breathe—why? I couldn't put my finger on it. Something was troubling me—a rising feeling of disconnection, but there was something else, something other.

"They aren't all edible, Father. People make mistakes all the time."

My stomach hurt, but I couldn't move.

"What's *old news*?" she asked.

I couldn't answer.

"I went to the shop the other day to pick up those boots you ordered for me. Your computer was on. There was a file marked *Old News*, and I clicked on it."

Fuck.

"Do you want to see it?"

I couldn't move—my body refused to comply with my thoughts. I knew what the clip was—Marcy, naked in the bathroom. My go-to, restored to its former glory. And now Rachel had seen it. I'm an idiot. My breath caught. I threw up on the table.

"That's not gonna help you, Dad."

She wiped my mouth.

"Did Ambrose throw up when you poisoned him, or did he just go into seizures?"

I couldn't answer.

"You're a real creep, Pops. A real fucking creep. But I guess you already knew that. You've always been good at seeing yourself, haven't you?"

She tossed a picture of my father on the table, followed by one of my mother, and then a photo of Paula holding her as a baby.

"I applaud your suicide—the guilt over your mother, the poisoning of your father, and the death of your wife. You're an honorable man, Pops."

She picked up her phone, dialed emergency services, and turned on the tears. She was a good actress—no, she was great. I couldn't have played distress any better. As I seized and blacked out, I was proud of her.

Almost sorry I didn't die.

EPILOGUE

My Rachel, after the proper amount of grief, paid a visit to Blackman, Devers, and Kroft, where she was given the bad news. She was to work until she was fifty-five. Her father was to remain on the respirator until he died a natural death. And she was to attend therapy.

The Wallace's have a history of mental illness, they said, and while she may not feel its effects now, a good therapist—of Greenwood's choosing—would be assigned to her.

Dr. Waddle had left her a voicemail.

They placed me by my father—side by side, our machines breathing and pumping. I wondered if he was conscious too—if he was lying there, glad at my situation, angry about his wife, and wishing he could take his belt to me one more time.

I'm not a bright man.

I look for patterns and words, but when they appear before me, I'm too dull to recognize there importance. *"I guess it runs in the family, Dad."* Could she have made it any clearer?

After a few months, I was more asleep than conscious. After a year, I barely thought at all. I guess it was a blessing.

I dreamed sometimes.

My hands were covered with blood, but it was not unpleasant. I had the feeling that it was okay, that my parents were nearby, and they knew what I was up to. There was a box on a table—fine wood grain and burnished top. I opened it and extracted a penis—thick and hard. It had been severed at the base. The blood on my hands was my own, and when I held the member to my groin, it reattached, and I was a new man.

I felt breath on my cheek. A figure standing behind me put his arms around me and pulled me close. He whispered:

"Hey, Wessy, you remember when I told you that remorse didn't last?" His voice was low, intimate. "Let's get the fuck out of here."

For the first time in seven years, I blinked my eyes.